Seth

Cyborgs: More Than Machines, #5

Eve Langlais

Copyright © January 2014, Eve Langlais
Cover Art by Amanda Kelsey © January 2014
Edited by Devin Govaere
Copy Edited by Amanda L. Pederick
Produced in Canada

Published by Eve Langlais
1606 Main Street, PO Box 151
Stittsville, Ontario, Canada, K2S1A3
http://www.EveLanglais.com

ISBN-13: 978-1495305917
ISBN-10: 1495305910

Seth is a work of fiction and the characters, events and dialogue found within the story are of the author's imagination and are not to be construed as real. Any resemblance to actual events or persons, either living or deceased, is completely coincidental.

No part of this book may be reproduced or shared in any form or by any means, electronic or mechanical, including but not limited to digital copying, file sharing, audio recording, email and printing without permission in writing from the author.

Prologue

Seth fell in love while perched atop a climbing wall during a military endurance training exercise. Not exactly the most romantic of spots considering the braced four-by-four hunks of wood towering twelve feet high were gray and weather beaten, a nasty splinter waiting to happen for those with delicate skin. It wasn't a particularly nice day either with ominous clouds spread across the sky, heavy with moisture, threatening those running the dreaded course with a cold downpour.

But, despite it all, this was the place and time the course of his future changed forever.

Slender fingers, with short, rounded nails, clawed at the top of the structure where he sat with his legs dangling. For those who wondered, it wasn't laziness that kept him there or fear nor even fatigue. He could have easily leapt down and continued on his way, but he held himself back to help those who struggled once they reached this part of the race.

His altruistic streak would cost him the distinction of coming in first, but Seth preferred to fly under the radar. It wasn't that he couldn't win—*I so could kick everyone's ass*—but, life had taught him that excelling and finishing first in everything didn't ingratiate him with his peers. Heck, he'd gotten into fights because of his achievements. Won those too. But it didn't earn him any friends, so when he enlisted in the military, he chose to follow a different path than that of superstar. He became a middle-of-the-pack kind of guy. The fellow who sacrificed glory to help out another recruit, which, in an unexpected bonus, resulted in him often scoring a free beer or two later on at the bar.

But back to the love of his life about to make her appearance. His first glimpse of her was those distinctly feminine fingers. Without asking, he wrapped his hand around her slim wrist and heaved the woman until she could balance herself on the slim peak. Most recruits, while surprised at his chivalry, managed to mutter a "thank you" at his unexpected aid. Not this gal.

Sparking blue eyes framed by thick lashes glared at him. "What the hell do you think you're doing?" she asked.

"Giving you a helping hand."

"I don't need help. I am perfectly capable of climbing the wall on my own."

The acerbic statement was uttered from perfect Cupid's bow lips. "I never said you weren't. I was just being a gentleman."

"A gentleman?" She arched a dark brow. "I see. You helped me because I'm a woman. That's sexist."

He laughed. "Guy, girl, it doesn't matter. I help everybody. I'm just a *giving* kind of guy." And he'd love to give to her, preferably somewhere private with a bed.

She chose to ignore his subtle innuendo. "Did I look like I needed help?"

Actually, she'd scrambled up with ease even before he gave her a hand. "No. But it would be rude for me not to offer when I do with everyone else. The wall is hard for some. I see no point in letting my fellow soldiers tire themselves out when I can spot them."

She regarded him with suspicion. "You mean to tell me you sit here and haul everyone over?"

"Just about. Except for Charlie." Because if Seth attempted to haul that almost seven foot behemoth over the wall, he risked rupturing something vital.

A tiny smile curved her lips. "I'm pretty sure Charlie can just step over the wall. Anyhow, thanks, I guess."

"My pleasure. Are you new?"

"Just transferred in from a base down in Texas. But I don't have time to chat. I've got to get moving if I'm going to finish in the top ten."

"You actually care about that? You do know so long as we pass the course, we're good."

"I know; however, the rumor mill says the top runners in today's endurance contest will get a shot at a special project."

His interest perked. "I didn't hear anything about any special projects." Which surprised him. Seth prided himself on being a fount of information.

She hopped to the ground, knees bending to absorb the impact. "Not surprising. It's pretty hush-hush because apparently finding out about it is another part of the test. Or so I hear," she threw over her shoulder with a full-lipped grin before jogging off.

The knowledge that there was a secret assignment looking for recruits shouldn't have bothered him. Seth wasn't into being selected for special projects. Those usually meant more work. More responsibility. More shit to rain down if things went to hell. He'd rather be just one of the plain Joe's, sucking back a brew at the end of the week, keeping his commanding officer happy.

So if that was the case, why exactly was he leaping down from the wall and ignoring the newest arrival hunched over at its base, huffing and puffing? Could it be the waggle of a perfect heart-shaped ass? The captivating features of a cutie with long dark hair bound in a ponytail? Or the unspoken taunt that she was better than him?

Nah. More like the curiosity that killed the cat. Seth couldn't stand not knowing a secret. If the military was planning something, he wanted in on it and if it got him closer to a certain hottie … then he was showing officer potential in the form of multi-tasking. Booyah!

As for his teasing wave as he sped by her, determined to finish first? Yeah, that he did just to annoy her.

Chapter One

Years and years later, on the planet cyborgs called home ...

The mission was a success. The crew of the *SSBiteMe* returned in triumph with one of the long lost female cyborgs in tow. In a twist that showed the universe's perverse sense of humor, Bonnie, the rescued female previously known as B785, happened to be Chloe's sister. For those not in the know, Chloe was the first female cyborg they'd ever found. She was currently partnered with the cyborg leader, Joe. The two made a cute couple, and for someone like Seth, who enjoyed teasing, offered so many opportunities for outspoken comments, which in turn led to some exercise as Joe tried to teach him some manners, usually with his fists.

Good times. But back to Bonnie and the sisterly reunion. Man, did that cause some chaos and tears, which Aramus of course complained about. That grumpy bastard seemed convinced the happy siblings would cause irreparable rust to their machine parts.

Joe was understandably pleased at the *SSBiteMe*'s finding. Every female cyborg they rescued was a point in their favor against the military that abused them. An impromptu celebration was planned, but Seth didn't stick around to try out the new alcoholic brew his brothers had managed to create during his absence.

A little glum, Seth left the family reunion behind before anyone saw the moisture glistening in his eyes or heard him sniffle. Sometimes, his human side was all too strong. All too envious.

Where's a real damned bar when you need one? A few gallons of whiskey would have proven welcome right about now. However, other than the occasional experimental fermentation, alcoholic beverages weren't something they had in stock. Nor was it high on the list of priorities when they went raiding and trading.

Darned practical cyborgs with their list of required supplies that included things like refined metals, fabric, and computer parts. While they might have thrown off the chains enslaving them to humans, his cyborg brethren had yet to remember what it meant to live. What it felt like to embrace fun and joy. To do things for the simple sake of pleasure.

They were a dour bunch at times, logical in their reasoning, serious in their interactions, and sometimes maddening as they struggled to not let their machine side overcome the man. Yet, despite their flaws, and perhaps because of their struggles with them, Seth loved them all, even when they proved irrational.

Blame the fact that, unlike some of the solider models, his cybernetic version, that of undercover operative, got to keep many of his human traits. Lucky, or not, depending on the view, Seth remembered his past life and was in touch with his humanity. He felt all too much. While he might sport the latest technology and software in his

BCI—which stood for brain computer interface—in his case, the man never lost control to his machine. *I live. I breathe. I feel ...*

Leaving his celebrating brothers behind, and in search of solitude, Seth headed for the forest, in need of its calming influence. He couldn't exactly pinpoint the reason for his depression. Their recent mission had proven both satisfying and trying.

Einstein, a good friend of his, had not only found a missing cyborg female, he'd fallen for her, hard. By all the nanos in his body, Seth wished his buddy Einstein well, he truly did. It was beyond awesome that his all-too-serious friend had discovered love, an emotion that made life worth living. Yet, it was times like these, times when he saw others moving on with the future, that he wished, weak as it made him sound, that he could also find the same kind of joy, and acceptance. That he too could find someone to share life's ups and downs with. It didn't help he'd had it once before, lost it because of circumstances outside his control, and had yearned for it ever since.

Knowing of the possibility, the nirvana the right person could bring to his life made watching others achieve it so much harder. Had he lost his chance? Or just not found it yet?

Maybe one day my turn will come. Again.

Of course, he didn't expect it to happen so quickly.

There was no warning. No sound to betray their presence. No smell. Nothing. Just the sudden cold touch of a pistol muzzle nudging the back of his head.

He froze.

Silence reigned except for the chirp of the little creatures that lived in the woods and emitted bird-like noises. They sounded cute until you came across them. Unlike a feathered denizen of earth, the furry buggers who chirped like songbirds resembled more a rat with spiked fur, razor-sharp teeth, and a really bad attitude if they felt threatened. Ankles beware!

They're not the only ones who get nasty when their lives are in danger.

Although none of his muscles moved, Seth held himself ready to act, letting his internal processor analyze the space around him, seeking a hint, anything to give him an edge. He inhaled deep, testing the air, in an attempt to see if he could identify his attacker. Lo and behold, he got a faint trace.

Of all the things he expected to smell out here in the forest, vanilla soap wasn't one of them. The clean fresh scent was familiar, as was the position he found himself in. Strange as it seemed, he'd lived the almost exact scenario once, a long time ago. But he'd thought that person dead. Or at least lost to him. *It can't be. Not after all this time.* Was it possible?

No time like the present to test his theory.

"Well hello there, gorgeous. I knew you couldn't resist me forever." He couldn't help but grin when his guess was confirmed by a husky voice that still had the ability to send shivers down his spine.

"I see you're still just as annoying.

Whirling lightning quick, Seth played the part of surrendering victim and held his hands above his head so the gun pointed at his forehead. Face to face, he couldn't help but drink in the reality of the lady who haunted his dreams. His ex-partner. The only woman he'd ever loved. The only one who ever spurned him. The woman he'd once called wife.

A wife who wore a scowl and didn't shower him with welcoming kisses.

He couldn't resist goading her. "Me, annoying? Never. Handsome and dashing, yes. I might even use the term rakish."

"And cocky. You do realize I'm holding a loaded gun to your head. Do you really want to tempt me into pulling the trigger?"

If she'd wanted him dead, his brains would already decorate the bushes around them. Anastasia knew hundreds of ways to kill a man. However, he'd wager she wouldn't have returned just to put a bullet in his head. She'd torture him first. Probably painfully. How he'd missed her.

"You won't kill me," he stated with utter confidence.

"Don't be so sure. I've pictured your death a thousand times. My favorite was the one where I push you off that cliff we once climbed in the Himalayan Mountains and watch you fall, knowing that you'll actually have time to reflect on what a jerk you are before you hit the ground."

Okay, so this wasn't exactly the reunion he'd once hoped for. Someone still had anger issues. Question was, did she mean it when she said she wished him dead? Only one way to find out.

"Well, if you've returned to kill me, would you mind getting on with it? I've got places to go, people to see."

"You mean irritate." The muzzle of her gun dropped, and she rolled her expressive blue eyes.

"And here I thought you enjoyed my quirky nature and sense of humor."

"I blame my previously defective, human brain for that momentary lapse of reasoning."

He couldn't help but laugh. "Oh how I've missed your acerbic tongue. My dearest Anastasia, love of my life, I am delighted you've returned to brighten my existence. Did you miss me?"

She snorted. "Like a dog misses his fleas."

No longer in fear for his life, Seth clasped his hands to his chest. "Be still my racing heart. Your romantic words are a balm to this wounded soul. For so long I've—"

"Oh would you stop with the theatrics. I'm here on serious business."

"What could be more serious than saving our marriage and rekindling our love for each other?" He spoke in jest, but inside, despite the illogicalness of it, he couldn't help but hope that she'd missed him and that she had indeed returned to give him another chance.

"Love? Ha. I remember your version of love. Unfortunately for me, it didn't include fidelity."

Not that old argument again. "How many times must I tell you? Nothing happened." The truth. A pity she never believed it.

"I found you both naked in bed."

"I was set up."

"Not that again. Are you still trying to pull that bullshit? I would have thought you'd have come up with a better excuse, or at least an apology for being a two-timing jerk."

"For the last time, I did nothing wrong." Stubbornness had nothing to do with it. He wouldn't ask forgiveness for something he was not guilty of. In his mind, she was the one who owed him an apology for not trusting in him or his word.

Anastasia let out a disparaging sound. "Not according to Natasha."

Natasha. Just the mention of her name was enough to have Seth seeing red. The Russian spy had disappeared after her frame job, the one that saw Anastasia leaving him for good. Nothing he could say would change her mind. Hell, she'd almost killed him for his supposed treachery. Was it any wonder he accepted the deep space mission the military sent him on? That he pretended their new programming had wiped his memories. He'd wanted to forget how the love of his life preferred to believe a lie instead of him.

It seemed some things hadn't changed. Some of his elation at her appearance faded, and a weariness entered his tone when he asked, "Why are you here, Anastasia?"

Face scrunched in an expression of distaste, she spat out the words he'd waited forever to hear. "I need you."

Despite her recent adamant stance that there was nothing left between them, he couldn't help but taunt her. "I'm yours. I guess the next question is, with foreplay or without? Naked or dressed? I've got a bed back at the compound, but if you'd prefer to remain unseen, I'm not averse to a little backwoods nookie."

Her lips tightened into a thin line of annoyance. It did nothing to detract from her attractiveness, their fullness envied by those who relied on Botox for the same look. "I don't need you for sex, you idiot. I need you for a mission."

Of course she did. Anastasia always did make work her first priority. Known by the military as Unit S100, she was the first female cyborg spy model—and a secret he'd long held, even from his brothers.

Separated years ago, after that bloody misunderstanding, he'd just about given up hope on ever seeing her again. He'd even wondered if she still lived, given the war humans had declared on cyborgs.

He should have known better. Anastasia was a tough cookie. If anyone could emerge intact from the cyborg fiasco and land on her feet, it was her. He wondered how she'd survived. What she'd had to do. In his quest for freedom and to aide his fellow cyborg brothers, Seth had to kill more than he liked.

While his human side lamented the blood he'd shed, his machine side, that analytical part of him that could separate emotion from cold hard facts, recognized that what the human military did and continued to do was wrong. It helped keep the nightmares at bay when he was forced to get rough and blood flowed like a river. Not his of course.

But the military didn't give him any other option. It was kill or be killed. Unfortunately for them, he was good at the latter. And the humans had only themselves to blame.

Cyborgs hadn't become machines by choice. They hadn't volunteered to give up their freedom or humanity. They had their choices and free will taken away by force. Or at least the majority of them had. A few, like Seth and Anastasia, chose their fate and went into it eyes wide open, thinking they did the world a favor and that they were on the side of the greater good. Once he'd learned differently, Seth sided with those he felt most closely attuned to. The underdogs. The downtrodden and abused. His cyborg brothers.

It seemed Anastasia had finally bucked the military machine too, and now, here she was, in the flesh. Her lovely, curvy flesh.

A part of him wanted to hate her for not believing him all those years ago. He wanted to say he no longer gave a damn about what had happened during that time or if she missed him. He should tell her screw what she needed and send her on her jealous way. He didn't.

All it took was seeing her again and all the feelings he'd hidden and tried to overcome came rushing back. It was more than just her looks, which had remained virtually unchanged. Sure she sported a slightly shorter hairstyle, the dark tresses traded in for blonde ones. But while hair color was changeable, the essence of her, the fine bone structure, the eyes, remained the same. Her face might have acquired a hardness that she'd lacked in her youth, but at her core, she was still Anastasia, the woman he'd loved and touched and worshipped.

The one he'd spoon fed chunky chocolate ice cream to in bed. The one he'd learned ballroom dancing for. The one he'd sprinted to catch after their chance meeting on a wall. The reason he'd become who he was today. The only woman he'd ever given a damn about. The only woman to make even his mechanical heart race and his cock go wild.

Fuck me, I still love her. He'd probably never stopped. *Actually, I know I never did.* And it wasn't for lack of trying.

Once he'd come to grips with the fact he'd never see Anastasia again, he'd tried to erase her from his mind—and heart. He'd slept with other women. Human women. Enhanced women. Even droids in brothels. He came. It wasn't as if losing her meant he'd gotten impotent or unaffected by erotic touch. He easily eased the needs of his body, but nothing cured the needs of his heart. No one else could compare to the beautiful, maddening, highly intelligent, oh-so-dangerous woman before him.

Curse her for being so damned glorious.

And curse him for being unable to stop himself from saying, "I'll help. I just need to tie up a few things before we go. Why don't you follow me back to our base so I can let my brothers know I'm taking off."

She shook her head. "No pit stops to the base. We don't have time. We have to leave now before anyone notices I'm here."

"What's the rush?"

"I can't say."

"You won't even allow me a moment to pack a bag?"

"Everything you could possibly need is already on board."

"What if I need to water my plants?"

"The only thing growing in your home is the mold in your bathroom."

"You seem rather well informed."

"It's my job."

Anastasia still spied? More and more curious. "I can't just up and leave. My friends deserve to be told."

"We don't have the time it would take for you to go back and explain things." She tapped her foot in impatience.

"Maybe not in person, but I can at least send Joe a wireless BCI to BCI message."

"If you must." She didn't utter a long-suffering sigh, but the tone of her reply adequately relayed her annoyance at his insistence.

"You're too kind," was his sarcastic reply.

As Seth followed the familiar swagger of Anastasia's ass as she weaved through the trees—while recalling said ass in less-clothed circumstances—he sent a mental probe out to Joe, the de facto leader of the cyborg liberation.

Hey, boss.

Seth. Where are you? We're having a bit of a mini party here, and I, for one, could use your brand of humor to counteract Aramus' scowl.

Nothing short of a lobotomy will fix that man's attitude. Although Seth often did wonder whether Aramus would lighten up if he met the right woman. Of course, said woman would have to be deaf, and of the blow-up variety, else she'd never tolerate his acerbic tongue. Fingers crossed the one he'd ordered his ornery friend for Christmas would brighten his outlook on life. She could supposedly suction a golf ball through fifty feet of hose and was programmed to say only three things. "Yes, dear." "How may I serve you?" And a specialty phrase Seth specifically requested the sex shop's bestselling girlfriend model to say after sex, "Seth's dick is bigger than yours is."

Seth couldn't wait to hear Aramus' bellow of outrage the first time he heard it.

Where are you? Joe asked, interrupting his train of thought.

Off in the woods, about to leave the planet.

Leave? With who? And on what ship? My processor shows no active missions on the roster.

That's because this is a secret mission.

Secret from me? Joe might have spoken only in his mind, but Seth could imagine the growl.

An old friend showed up and asked for my help.

Which old friend and what kind of help?

I'm not sure yet. They haven't said much, just that I'm needed.

It didn't take long for Joe's analytical mind to grasp the most important facet of their conversation. *Wait a second. When you say old friend, are you implying someone off planet has requested your aid?*

Depends what you mean by off planet.

Seth! Joe practically shouted his name.

The person in question is not a current member of our community and made the request in person.

You mean you're with them? Right now? But how? I'm showing no vessels in the immediate area. Actually, none of our reports show any activity other than from our own ships. What the hell is going on, Seth?

Hearing the irritation in his friend's voice, Seth frowned. He liked Joe and respected him. It didn't sit well keeping secrets from him. He'd kept enough secrets already. "Oh, wifey poo, Joe wants to know who you are and how you got past our detection systems. What should I tell him?"

"First off, I am not your wife."

"I never signed divorce papers."

"It only takes one well aimed bullet to become a widow."

"What a waste of ammo though."

She tossed him a glare. "Secondly, you can't tell him anything."

"I have to tell him something."

"Tell him it's classified information."

"Yeah, that's not going to fly. And Joe deserves better than that from me."

She sighed. "You and your friends. Can't you ever just say no?"

"Lucky for you I can't, or I wouldn't be following you on the basis of your so nicely put request for my aide."

"Lives are at stake."

"If that's the case, then all the more reason why we should enlist Joe and the others to help."

"We can't. Where we need to go, they won't fit in."

"What do you mean not fit in?" Understanding dawned. "We're going undercover and posing as humans." The ability to blend in was one of the main reasons cyborg spy models got to retain their humanity instead of undergoing the reprogramming and desensitization the other units went through. *Or I could call it what it was. Torture.* Intense bouts of torture and sensory deprivation, along with memory wipes and strict programming, took perfectly good people and made them machines, tools for the military to use. Expendable forces that would march to their deaths and not say a word in protest. Until the day their programming failed and the machines fought back.

"I can understand why you can't use them, but I need to tell Joe something. Surely there is something he and the others can do so they don't come looking and digging for me. He won't just accept my leaving without some kind of answer."

"Actually, there is one thing he and the others can do because it doesn't look like I'll have time to take care of it myself. Tell him to go to the following coordinates." She rattled off a stream of numbers, which he stored.

"What's there?"

"Answers."

"Just that? Answers. He's going to want more than that."

"I can't tell you more than that."

Seth made a face. "Let me guess, it's classified."

"Just tell him to go. And quickly. Oh, and he might want to do so carefully. He'll find some answers there, but they won't come easy."

Now Seth was intrigued. A mystery adventure with danger. Sounded like fun. Pity he already had plans elsewhere. Then again, given his current companion, he doubted his mission would lack for fun and games.

Joe, my contact says if you want answers and some action you should head to ... He recited off the coordinates, only once. Their BCI had perfect recall. Once told something, it remained stored in their databanks forever.

Got it, but do you mind telling me what we're going to find?

No idea. My contact says it's classified info. He couldn't quite hide his disgruntlement. *Apparently, though, you should expect resistance, so tell whoever's going to be careful.*

Funny how even a wireless transmission could relate a snort of amusement. *Subtlety isn't Aramus' strong suit, but if there's something to be found, then he'll ferret it out. Are you sure you're okay? If you need me to come rescue you ...*

I'm fine, dude. You just take care of my cyborg family while I'm gone. I'll be back before you know it. Hopefully with Anastasia. Make that definitely with Anastasia.

Seth made a vow in that moment, an unspoken promise to himself that there was no military or force in the universe that would keep him from her side. Whether she liked it or not. He'd almost wager on the not.

Chapter Two

Anastasia resisted the urge to peer over her shoulder, even though the skin at her nape prickled. She could feel Seth following, feel him with every extrasensory perception she had. Even without looking, she'd have wagered one thing. *I'll bet he's checking out my ass.* It was what he always did, and once upon a time, she'd loved it. Until she realized hers wasn't the only ass he kept an eye on.

Jealousy was a vicious bitch. Anastasia had never met the emotion until Seth, and once she and the green-eyed mistress got acquainted, she found her hard to shake, especially when it came to the handsome recruit.

Young and usually so focused, Anastasia couldn't help but find herself flattered by Seth's ardent attention—who wouldn't? He was the equivalent of the captain of the football team. Tall, fit, blond, good-looking, with a smile to charm even the most hardened of battle axes to give him a free pass when caught outside of the barracks after curfew.

When he turned his attention to her, Anastasia couldn't help but blossom, and crave it. Not that she gave in easy or let him know. The fact that she'd found herself instantly attracted to him from the first moment they met made her suspicious. What kind of idiot sat on a wall and waited to help others in a race to see who was best? Seth did. Or would have if she'd not teased him with the knowledge of a prize for the top winners that day. When he blew past her on the endurance course with a cockily thrown, "See you at the finish line", she became determined to show him she was just as good as him. Maybe even better. The end result?

They'd both been chosen for a special mission. As a matter of fact, they became an unstoppable duo, in the field and the bedroom. Unfortunately, it wasn't until after they tied the knot that she realized hers wasn't the only bedroom he visited.

Set up my ass. She couldn't believe he clung to that lie even after all these years. She'd seen the proof. Heard it as well in full moaning embarrassment. Nothing like getting handed a video of your husband naked in a bed with a beautiful woman straddling him to shatter a dream.

When her commanding officer gave her the order to terminate Seth's lying ass, she'd gladly jumped at the chance to do something to hurt him back. The pain, oh god, the pain of his betrayal had cut her to the bone. Heart ripped out, stomped on, set on fire and burnt to ash, she'd thought herself cried out when she went to deliver his punishment. Wrong. Tears ran down her cheeks the entire way there. She'd sobbed despite her anger.

She blamed her eventual failure to terminate him on her emotional weakness. She'd hesitated, and he ended up getting away. For the first time in her career, she'd failed a mission.

Returning to base, dejected and head hanging in shame, she'd expected to get severely reprimanded for not completing her task. But the same military officer who showed such sorrow at breaking the bad news of her husband's infidelity showed an almost smug satisfaction when she announced her inability to take out the traitor.

She never knew what happened to her cheating jerk of a husband other than he lived. Despite her determination to pretend he'd never existed, she still heard through the grapevine that the military ended up canceling their plan to kill him. He got reassigned to a different base. After only a little argument on her part, she had her defective heart removed and replaced with a newer mechanical one, one that, despite its efficiency, still emitted the occasional ghostly ache. Time passed, and despite the fact they worked in theory for the same government, she never saw Seth again.

She also never officially got a divorce either but more because things went to hell in a hand basket after her voluntary decision to join the cybernetic special ops group. As an integral part of the cyborg program, and nosy when it came to certain inconsistencies that began cropping up, she caught wind early on of the plan to eliminate all cyber units.

The nerve. And after all she'd given to the military.

Before they could send a force to exterminate her, she wiped herself out. She faked her death. It wasn't that hard, not with the resources and skills they'd given her. Determined to survive, she proceeded to remove every trace of her existence from every single database and hard drive she could hack into. She set fires to rooms with hard paper copies. She eliminated a few key players, military asshats she'd never cared much for in the first place. Anastasia cleaned the slate and started over.

Anna Kline was born. And Anna followed a new prime directive. Contrary to what Seth and the others did, which was to find and free as many cyborgs as possible without getting caught, she went after bigger fish. She wanted the ones who'd created the program in the first place. The ones who'd bankrolled the project, ordered the unlawful recruitment, and pulled the plug when their toys didn't behave as told.

She went into deep undercover and, in the process, discovered more than she bargained for. In an odd twist, she also stumbled upon Seth's file. It seemed her *husband* had been a busy machine. Part of the cyborg rebellion force. A wanted criminal by the human federation, the military, and pretty much everyone who wanted to eradicate the cyborgs. A man to admire. A man capable of making her metal heart malfunction.

He was also the perfect tool to get her to the next stage of her operation.

Much as it galled her, she knew of no one else with the skills to help her. Or who could be counted on to protect not just her but also certain cyborgs in custody.

"How did you get to the surface without Joe and the others detecting you?" Seth asked, derailing her thoughts.

"Cloaking device."

"The new one the military's been using?"

"You're aware of it?"

"We've encountered it. And some of their new damned tracking bugs. What gives with the technology? Einstein's never seen anything like it. We can't even detect the shit unless we're looking right at it, and even then, our processors insist it's not there."

"There've been some breakthroughs since your group splintered off."

"Say it like it is. We escaped execution."

"I prefer the term mutiny."

"And you're ignoring my initial query. The cloaking tech. Something like that was probably years in the making. How did we not hear of it? Even now, there's not a whisper anywhere, not even in hacker circles. It's like these new abilities to cloak bugs, and even ships, came out of nowhere."

Seth wasn't asking the right question. "Not nowhere." Just elsewhere.

He didn't catch her implication, so she didn't feel a need to explain.

"So who did you steal your device from?" he asked.

"I didn't have to steal it. I borrowed it."

His rich laugh sent shivers dancing in places that hadn't felt a quiver in so long she'd forgotten they existed. "Okay then, where did you *borrow* it from?"

"Let's just say my current mission gives me access to certain things, like this ship."

"What ship?"

She sent a mental command to her vessel, and in the seemingly empty clearing, it shimmered into existence. Hovering above the ground, the stasis field, which kept it aloft, barely stirred the lush aqua colored grassy fronds topped with speckled green and white flowers.

"Holy shit. I never even knew it was there," Seth exclaimed.

"It's a great feature, but it requires a lot of power to maintain, just like keeping it off your planetary radars sucks up juice, so, if you don't mind, we should get going."

"Your wish is my command, wife."

"Would you mind not calling me that?" she snapped. "I'd rather the crew not know about our marital situation, which I intend to resolve by the way."

"Crew? What crew?"

"I'll debrief you once we're away from the cyborg planet and on our way to the rendezvous point."

"More and more intriguing. You know how I enjoy a good mystery and a challenge."

Indeed she did. After all, it was how they'd ended up together in the first place.

Chapter Three

Years ago, on a training base on earth …

Anastasia finished third, just ahead of several other recruits in tiptop shape. She struggled not to pant, having sprinted the last half mile in order to secure her spot. She never did catch the guy from the wall who had effortlessly outpaced her. She found him, though, as she crossed the last hurdle.

Chatting with a pretty sergeant while sipping from a canteen, he didn't even appear as if he'd exercised. No heavy breathing or giant wet armpit stains. Not that she bore any either. Her antiperspirant was heavy duty and lathered on, but still, given he'd beaten her and the others by a fair stretch, he should have borne some sign of strain. The jerk.

Catching her evil glare, he tossed her an easy grin along with his canteen. She caught it one handed and hesitated only a moment before unscrewing it to drink. The flutter in her tummy had nothing to do with the fact she drank from the same bottle his lips had touched. She was too mature at twenty for such a girlish reaction. But she wasn't above petty jealousy that demanded she do something violent to the perky blonde sergeant when she took a bite from her protein bar and offered golden boy the rest.

As if sensing her irritation, he winked in her direction. Just that. A single wink then turned away and ignored her. Good. Because his disinterest, whether feigned or not, made things easier. Anastasia had a firm policy of no fraternizing with other recruits, and not just because the military policies mandated it. Everyone knew it was just asking for trouble to screw people you had to work and live with every day.

Sidling over to a shady spot, she enjoyed the few moments of respite allowed as those in charge waited for the rest of the recruits to come straggling across the finish line. Big ol' Charlie was last, kind of. Slow and steady, he lumbered to the finish line, but he didn't arrive alone. He toted a red-faced wheezing body slung over one shoulder.

With everyone done the grueling course, their lieutenant took charge. "Attention!" he bellowed. Bodies scrambled to line up. Feet slammed together. Hands shot straight down to their sides. Gazes focused ahead.

It didn't matter that they'd done this in seconds. Their CO still berated them. "You have got to be the sorriest excuses for recruits I've ever seen," yelled the lieutenant. "If I had my way, I'd kick all your asses out. As it is, I'm feeling lenient today. Three laps around the quad for all of you."

Ah damn. She knew better than to groan aloud at the punishment. Someone else though hadn't gotten the memo. A single whine followed the announcement.

The lieutenant smiled, an evil grin, as he said, "Make that four laps, you lazy laggards. Dismissed."

With crisp salutes, the group dispersed. A bunch immediately set off at a sedate jog. Anastasia made to follow but stopped as the lieutenant barked her name along with several others. "Privates Seth Murray. Horace Dempsen. Anastasia Kettle." One by one, the ten people he called halted and spun around to line up in front of their commanding officer.

Anastasia did a mental fist pump. All the names called had finished in the top ten of the endurance run. She wondered if the rumor about the secret mission was true. She also wondered which of the names belonged to Captain America. If they were called in order of arrival, then that would make him Seth. As if she cared. As far as she was concerned, he was the competition. The only interest she had in him was how to beat his ass in the next round of whatever test the military would choose to subject them to.

Hopefully, a mental one. When it came to smarts, Anastasia didn't worry. Much. With the military, a person never knew what to expect. They were known for breaking even the proudest recruit down and rebuilding them into the perfect soldier.

"You ten need to follow me." No explanation. No clue as to why. Just an order to follow.

It was then Anastasia noted they had company. A short little man, his wispy hair combed over a prominent bald spot, wearing in an ill-pressed suit with rounded glasses perched on a pug nose, cleared his throat. The lieutenant turned and bent so that the newcomer could mutter something unintelligible. Whatever it was, the lieutenant didn't mind because he shrugged before he shouted,

"Private Passeaux, get your fat ass back here. You're needed too."

Curious. Charlie, the behemoth, was the only one in their group who hadn't finished in the upper group. But no one could doubt the strength of his body. *I just hope the next test doesn't involve arm wrestling, or I'm screwed.*

In single file, they marched after the lieutenant, while the guy in the suit quick-walked to keep up. He took them through the training grounds, past the barracks, and tortured them by ignoring the mess hall, where the wafting smell of food made her tummy grumble.

They trekked through a fair portion of the base to an unmarked building with a swipe pad bolted next to a thick metal door. The short civilian, or so she assumed given his lack of uniform, pulled forth a keycard from under his wrinkled button-up shirt. The chain it hung on had just enough slack for him to lean forward and scan it. With just the slightest whisper of sound, the door swung open.

That was only the first of the many security checkpoints. A pair of soldiers manned a square reception area upon entry. One by one, each recruit walked through a body scanner then stood still with arms over their head and legs akimbo for a pat-down. They went through this process three times before they reached a floor several levels underground. No one spoke a word, not even the few people they passed in the halls. Only the clomping of their combat boots broke the sterile silence.

Their journey ended at a nondescript door. This one just required a thumb reading from the bespectacled fellow. It slid open, and he gestured them in. Talk about anti-climactic. Anastasia gazed around at the practically empty white room with the dozen gray bucket seats bolted to the floor.

"Park your asses and be quiet until someone comes to get you." Brusque command given, the door slid shut behind their lieutenant and the balding man.

With shrugs and curious glances around, everyone grabbed a seat. Only the shuffle of clothing as they shifted position broke the stagnant quiet, for the first hour at least. Anastasia noted several of the men and the one other female tried to catch a few winks. Their eyes closed, their bodies relaxed, and one even snored.

How can they sleep?

Anastasia was too keyed up. *I wonder what's next. What do they want us for?*

Restless, her roving gaze touched on that of Captain America, or so she'd dubbed him. He slumbered as well. Or did he?

As if sensing her glance, he stopped feigning slumber and his eyes popped open. She pretended to peek at a spot over his head. A curve of his lips indicated he'd caught her looking.

More minutes passed. Her tummy rumbled, the sound discernible but not alone. She and the other recruits had not eaten anything since breakfast, hours ago at this point.

Silence still prevailed, and Anastasia tired of it. *How long are they going to make us sit here doing nothing?*

And when are we going to get some food? She was getting close to the point where she'd settle for gnawing on her chair if it did something to ease the ache in her belly.

More time passed, and even those who'd slept began to fidget. And squirm. But no one quite dared to disobey the lieutenant's last order.

Captain America was the first to crack. He slapped his hands together, the stark sound explosive after all the quiet. "So, guys and gals. Exactly what do you think they want with us?"

No one said a word, although Anastasia was tempted to "shhh" him. Something about the place they found themselves in was creepy. Despite the fact that the walls seemed like seamless white panels, she'd have wagered someone watched and listened. For all she knew, how they acted was the next part of their test.

Apparently, Captain America didn't hold the same theory, or he didn't care. "Lively bunch, I see. I'm Seth, by the way, for those who don't know me yet. I like drinking beer. Darts. Corny horror movies and the ladies." He tossed her a smile that highlighted a slight dimple in his cheek.

Again, no one dared reply, but she saw some of the group peer around, eyes anxious, as if they expected retaliation for his speech to come out of nowhere. Personally, she did too. She just made sure not to show it.

"Wow. You guys are a tough crowd. Or as my dad would say, Baaah." Whatever the joke, he found it funny, or so his amused snicker indicated. Seth hopped up from his seat and stretched.

Anastasia envied him. Her ass had gone numb a while ago. The rule breaker paced over to the door, and he tried the handle. No surprise, it was locked.

When he knocked on it, to the cadence of "Shave and a Haircut", Anastasia couldn't help but hiss, "Would you sit down and shut up before you get us all in trouble?"

"She speaks! Be still my racing heart." Down to his knees he dropped, hands over the left side of his chest, eyes sparking with mischief.

"Stop it," she whispered.

"Or what? They'll starve us to death? Not tell us what's going on? Already happening, gorgeous." He sprang to his feet and spoke to the ceiling. "Hey, whoever's listening, do you mind sending us some food? We're starving in here. Something to drink, too, might be nice while we're waiting."

Before Anastasia could berate him again, a panel slid open in the wall, and a tray slid out with a white cardboard box. Seth snagged it and lifted the lid. He smiled. "Thank you," he called out.

He plopped down in a chair, package on his lap. From its depths, he pulled a cellophane wrapped sandwich.

She practically drooled as he sank his teeth in. *Is that ham I smell? And mustard?* She'd kill for a bite.

He must have caught her covetous stare because he offered her the other half. "Hungry? Have some."

Forget the order to stay sitting. She practically dove on the offered sandwich, like a piranha on fresh meat. Stale bread, processed cheese, and Spam made to smell like ham had never tasted so good.

As she chewed, she noted the others staring at Seth. A few actually looked murderous.

Seth pulled out another sandwich. "I have more. They sent enough for us all, if you're brave enough to get your asses out of those chairs and come to get them."

It seemed hunger was the key into getting them to disobey. As the food got passed around, the other recruits began to converse in low tones. Oddly enough, Seth wasn't one of them.

Placing the box on the floor, he left his seat once again, bottle of water in hand. She tracked him with her eyes as he paced the edges of the wall, seeming to stare at nothing.

Curious, she joined him. When he paused to gaze intently at a blank white spot, she couldn't help but ask, "What are you looking for?"

"A way out, of course."

"Are you nuts? The lieutenant told us to stay here."

"Indeed he did."

"So why are you looking to flout a direct order?"

"Because I think this is a test."

"What's a test?"

"This room. The waiting. Everything." He waved a hand vaguely to gesture around them.

"And what makes you think that?"

"Well, wasn't it you who initially told me that the endurance run was one phase?"

"Yes."

"Then how do you know this room isn't another?"

The word "because" stuck to her tongue. How did she know? "Because this is the military. They expect recruits to follow orders."

"And the regular recruits are. They're the ones running around the quad until they puke. I think whoever selected us wants something more."

"More, as in?"

"Take a look around. You might not know most of these people being new here, but I do. I know for a fact at least three of the folks in here have IQs greater than one thirty."

Make that at least four. At one forty-one, Anastasia scored high on the Mensa scale. "So they're looking for smart recruits."

"For the most part. Charlie is average, but he has other qualities. Like strength. Which is clue number two. Now I think they're looking for something else."

"You mean like most likely to cause trouble?" She couldn't help but smirk.

He didn't take offense. "Maybe. Or the person, or people, most likely to think outside of the box. In this case, a real box. I saw this in a movie once. This psycho killer put a bunch of people in a building and expected them to solve a series of puzzles in order to escape."

"I think you're talking about *Saw*, and I'd hardly equate the military and their selection process with a fictional killer."

"Ah, but it's not just the military running this gig, or weren't you paying attention as we made our way down here?"

Actually, she had. Despite its location, the installation they found themselves ensconced in had a high number of people dressed in lab coats over civvies. While the guarded checkpoints boasted military personnel, the few others they'd encountered with their coiffed hair, makeup, and lack of military bearing gave them away.

"So we're in some kind of research installation. It doesn't mean they want a bunch of recruits escaping and running amok."

"Then I guess you won't care to join me." Leaning against the wall, palm flat and fingers spread, he arched a brow as the section he touched lit up in the shape of his hand. A panel slid open, just large enough to crawl in.

"How did you know that was there?"

"I think the better question is why. Shall we?" He gestured gallantly at the opening, offering her first crack.

She hesitated. Stay and obey? Or take a chance he was right and move on to the next phase of testing?

"Tick tock," he teased.

She scrabbled in first, the duct big enough to crawl comfortably in. She heard him rather than saw him as he followed after.

"Where do you think this goes?" she whispered.

"My guess would be somewhere."

"Smartass."

"Finally, a compliment. Although, I must say, most women tend to comment on my looks, not my intelligence."

"You can add irritating to that list."

"Aw, admit it, gorgeous. You find me intriguing."

"If by intriguing you mean annoying enough that I'm distracted by the weirdness of the situation instead of plotting ways to kill you, then yes."

He laughed, which, in the close confines, echoed around her. She would have retorted, but it was at that moment the portal slid shut, encasing them in darkness. Damn.

"Well that sucks," Seth complained. "Now how am I supposed to check out your ass?"

Chapter Four

The Present.

The vessel Anastasia led Seth onto was a small cruiser, military in origin according to the insignia splashed on various consoles and painted on the outside, but the shape, material, and control panel to fly it was unlike anything he'd seen.

"Where did you get this baby?" Seth asked, emitting a low whistle of admiration.

"I told you, I borrowed it."

"From who?" he asked, despite having an inkling of the answer.

"The military."

"And I'll bet they want it back. How safe is this thing?" In other words, did this vessel bear one of those infamous untraceable tracking devices that would lead the human forces to the cyborg hideout?

"If you're worried about anyone from the government following me here, don't. Once the cloaking is enabled, even military ships equipped with the same technology can't see a damned thing. Your cyborg planet is safe. For now."

"What's that supposed to mean?"

"It means if I managed to find you, then how long do you figure before someone else does?"

Plopping himself into the co-pilot seat, Seth propped his feet on the console while Anastasia fiddled with the dials. "I wondered about that. How did you find us? We've been extremely careful. We keep the coordinates in our heads. We never head here straight from a raid or supply run. Survey reports list this place as uninhabitable. So how did you find us?"

"I'm a cyborg."

"And?"

"Another cyborg told me."

A snitch? That caught his attention. "Who? Who betrayed our secret?"

Her fingers paused in midair, whatever command she was in the midst of taking a backseat as she turned to face him. "Betrayed? How is it betraying for one cyborg to tell another where to find sanctuary?"

Wife or not, he didn't sugarcoat it. "No one, not even cyborgs we come across, are given that information until we've ascertained they don't pose a danger to us or the colony. They go through strict checks, and when possible, we perform a BCI mind sweep to check for possible embedded sleeper viruses and programming." Because, as they'd learned with Chloe, sometimes even the most benign beings could harbor secrets. And, sometimes, in spite of reclaiming their humanity, mental time bombs remained ticking within.

"You think I'm a spy?" She batted her lashes in a tactic meant to look innocent.

"Ha. I know you are."

"Maybe you do, but they don't. I've been very careful about covering my trail. The humans would kill me if they knew what I was."

"Just because you're hiding your identity doesn't mean I can trust you. Inadvertently or not, you wouldn't be the first cyber unit to betray our kind."

"Glad to see you think so little of me," she muttered, turning back to her console.

"Says the woman who wouldn't trust me." He couldn't help but voice the accusation. It seemed he'd not quite gotten over the past.

"I, at least, never left behind proof I was a lying, cheating whore."

He couldn't help but grit his teeth as he ground out, "And I keep telling you. I was framed."

"To what purpose?" She spun around, eyes flashing. "Explain that to me. Why would our government or military frame you, knowing that to do so would split up their most effective spy couple? Between the two of us, we solved more mysteries, ferreted out more secrets, and took care of more problems than the rest of their department combined."

"Exactly."

"That's your answer?" Both her brows arched.

"Yup. We were too good. Too awesome. They feared us. Feared what we might find out, especially once their plans to rid themselves of the cyborgs began to circulate around. They got scared that, together, we'd become an unstoppable team who would sabotage their plans to turn all cyber units into mindless slaves."

Her lips thinned into a clamped line.

"What? No retort. No denial that maybe I'm right?"

"Even if what you said was true, and I misjudged you, what's done is done. We can't go back in time and change things. I've changed. You've changed. We've both moved on with our lives."

Not exactly. Yes, Seth lived and worked and even played, but the one thing missing from his existence was sitting right beside him, trying to pretend their reunion didn't affect her.

He knew better. His sensors had no trouble tracking the way her heart hitched when the topic got too emotionally charged. His processor noted her core temperature rose when they accidentally brushed each other. *And I'll bet if I kiss her, she kisses me back.*

Screw running an analysis and prognosis of possibilities. There was one quick way to find out.

Leaning over, he grabbed her by the ponytail, catching her off guard. When she opened her mouth to protest, he slanted his mouth over hers, swallowing her protest.

By all the metal parts in his brain, but most especially by the fleshy ones left to him, he'd forgotten the beauty of kissing the woman he loved. The way her warm breath fluttered against his mouth, how her tongue loved to twine around his, a sinuous dance before she sucked it.

And her scent. Oh fuck, her scent. A musky aroma like no other, an outward sign of her arousal that she could never hide, and which made him hunger for more. He went to drag her onto his lap, all his senses turned on so he wouldn't miss a single pleasurable sensation. It was that fact that made her chomp of his lip so painful. He recoiled with a "What the hell?"

"Keep your mouth and hands to yourself."

"Why? You enjoyed it. I know you did."

"The reaction of my body is not the question. You have no right to take liberties with me." Pertly said and totally at odds with the flush in her cheeks, a sure sign she'd lost control for a moment to the passion that had always existed between them.

"I'll take whatever liberties I like. You're my wife." How good it felt to say that aloud. "I'll kiss you if I damn well like to." And more ...

"Almost ex-wife, and one who has a boyfriend. So, if you don't mind, keep your kissing to yourself, or I'll dump your ass in space."

He ignored the threat as the more important part of her statement filtered through.

A boyfriend? She had a boyfriend. *A BOYFRIEND!*

Even if Seth was more machine than man, it didn't matter. He still growled like a beast. "Not for long."

"What did you say?"

He shoved his jealousy into a ballroom-sized space in his BCI and slammed the door shut. Then hammered some boards over it. And then bricked it over. He smiled. "I said, I hope I get to meet the lucky guy before long."

So I can tear him apart and ship his pieces back to Einstein to use as spare parts. Illogical or not, no one touched his wife but him. No one.

Chapter Five

Only a blind idiot would have missed Seth's displeasure at her mention of a boyfriend. And only a complete liar would have denied to herself that she enjoyed his show of jealousy.

For a woman who'd moved on with her life and left her husband and past behind, she still took perverse pleasure in knowing it bothered him she'd taken up with another man. A human man. A nice man. *A boring idiot whose primary use is to help me keep my cover.* Not that she intended to reveal that to Seth. Let him suffer.

Besides, he'd soon have other things to worry about, such as her plans for him. Plans he surely wouldn't like.

"Now that we're out of reach of your cyborg friends, I guess it's time I told you what the goal is and why I need you."

"Given the fact you wanted to make sure I couldn't call for a rescue, I'm guessing I'm going to hate it. Does it involve me playing the role of an impotent arms dealer again?"

Anastasia couldn't help but chuckle. "Oh my god. I'd forgotten about that mission, and that barracuda of a woman."

Baroness Von Juger had dealt in illegal guns and collected pretty boys. In order to capture her attention, Seth dangled the most tempting bait ever, himself. Pretending he couldn't maintain an erection because of the trauma of losing his one true love, he'd proven irresistible to the mature lady. That poor woman plied him with oysters and aphrodisiacs, determined to have him, their failed trysts paving the way for Seth's so-called secretary, whom he dragged along everywhere, to snoop and gather the intel needed to convict the crooked cougar and net the US government a nice stash of goods.

A smile curved her lips in remembrance. "I'm afraid your role is not going to be as giggle worthy as that one."

"A shame. I rather enjoyed the party we had when we finished that assignment."

A party of two that involved champagne, a Jacuzzi tub, and the two of them naked. Seth had spent a marathon amount of passion-filled hours getting her back for every snicker and comment she made during his enforced chastity.

"I'm afraid your role is going to be more boring than that. You are going to become John Tweed, only survivor of a surveying duo sent to investigate a cluster of planets in this sector."

"Only survivor?"

"Your survey vessel crashed after entering the atmosphere, and while you walked away, your partner didn't. I just happened to find you on the planet due to a beacon signal when I did a sweep to see if the planet was viable for mining or stripping for resources."

"Good cover, except for the sector. To keep the cyborgs safe, we need to change it."

"Sorry, but we can't. My flight plan is already logged."

Seth didn't quite lose it, but he was pissed, something only those who knew him well would have recognized. The ticking vein in his forehead never did disappear, despite all his enhancements.

"You mean you logged a mission to this part of the galaxy knowing the cyborg planet was here? Are you completely defective or just being a bitch?"

"Seth, such language. And here I thought you wanted us to reconcile." She batted her lashes and smirked when he ground his teeth.

"Anastasia, this is no joking matter. There are a few hundred cyborgs on that planet whose lives you've just put in jeopardy."

"More like saved you mean. Or did it not occur to you that having your planet disappear from the annals and charts is more suspicious?"

"It occurred to us but, given the lack of traffic this way, deemed more acceptable than the risk of someone coming out for a peek at the planet with no info."

"Ah, but the planet now has info, thanks to John Tweed, who barely survived the savage jungle. Whom I nursed back to health after finding him dehydrated and practically starving. Oh, and your dissertation on the intelligent life you discovered, still in an early evolutionary phase, has placed said planet into protected status, which means no visitors and no random drive-bys less we affect the development of this newly discovered alien nation."

"You didn't."

"I did."

"You do realize that by placing the planet on a protected list you've ensured closer scrutiny on the comings and goings of that section of space. We already have a hard enough time getting supplies in. You've just made that job harder."

"Not if you start using the cloaking technology."

"Love to, but who's going to give us the cloaking schematics? Like you said, it's a closely guarded secret." His reply was rife with sarcasm.

"Which I have access to. Help me, and I'll give you everything you need to create your own cloaked vessels. Heck, I'm sure your friend Einstein can adapt it and use it to bubble your whole compound."

Knowing Einstein, he could probably hide the entire planet if given the right tools. "Excuse me if I don't say thank you yet. Because I'm sure there's more to this than you're telling me still."

"Why, John, I'm hurt."

"John." Seth snorted. "You named me after our imaginary dog?"

Dear John, their toy poodle and part of their cover during another mission. She couldn't help a wicked grin. "I thought it was apt. Anyway, as I was saying, *John*, I've rescued you, nursed you back to health, and am now bringing you back to the mother ship."

"Mother ship as in what? Science vessel? Galaxy Federation exploration? Private enterprise?"

Here was the part she couldn't hide any longer. The tidbit she'd intentionally hid knowing how he'd react. Or didn't. "A company research and experimentation vessel." Among other things.

"Infiltrating the enemy. Awesome."

"Awesome? That's all you have to say? I'm taking you aboard a vessel that is actively seeking our kind to run tests on. That has actually captured a few and—"

"What do you mean captured a few?"

An old human habit of hers reared its head. She twirled the ends of her hair around a finger and avoided his gaze. "Not all cyborgs were liberated or found their way to your planet."

"Duh. But the sentient ones were at least smart enough to hide."

"Those that escaped the military's clutches hid. Others were found, and not all of them were killed."

"You mean they kept some alive? Since when? I thought the military was exterminating all cyber units."

"They were, initially. Then, when our side began winning one too many skirmishes, the military changed its mandate from kill to capture. Those they get their hands on are shipped to the company and, there, under heavy guard, are used for experiments."

"Yeah, I'm aware of that. It happened to Joe a while back. They captured him during a raid and tried to torture him for info but didn't get anywhere. But they made it seem like he was an anomaly. And none of our digging has shown any orders or instructions to the contrary. As far as the world is concerned, cyborgs are to be destroyed on sight."

"What the world is told and what is actually happening are two vastly different things. I might also note that what Joe went through was nothing compared to what some others are being subjected to."

"We can't allow it to continue. We need to free the cyber units." How gallant he sounded. Yet, in this case, his chivalry was woefully misguided.

"Unfortunate as it is, they are not our primary objective."

"They might not be yours, but I won't stand by idly while one of my brothers is tortured."

"There's nothing you can do."

"Like bloody fucking hell!" The bellow from the usually sedate Seth took her by surprise. "These are people we're talking about, Anastasia. Our people. Worse than that, these poor soldiers didn't volunteer like you and I to become cyborgs."

"And their current dilemma is sad, but we need to look at the bigger picture."

"There is no bigger picture. They need our help. That should be our primary objective."

"Saving them will probably blow my cover and yours. I can't allow that. Not when I'm so close."

"And I'm telling you right now that, unless we do something to help them, you can count me out."

"You can't mean that."

"I can and do. If you've changed so much that you would rather sacrifice a few just for the sake of a mission, then I don't want to work with you. Or be with you. What happened to the girl I used to know? Despite the fact you were always climbing the next ladder, the woman I fell in love with wouldn't have let any job come between her and the right thing."

For some reason, his words stung. "That's not fair. I've helped plenty of cyborgs in the last few years. Hell, the mission I'm sending your friends on should save the lives of a couple if they're careful."

"And what of where you're taking me? How many cyborgs on board?"

"There are at least two in stasis."

He prodded. "And?"

She sighed. "One being used as a test subject."

"Testing what?"

"Ways to sedate us and get us back under control."

"Why do I get the feeling there's more?"

How well he knew her. She sighed. "They're also looking for a way to shut our nanos off."

His shocked expression said it all. Without the nanos coursing through their bodies, their metal parts and BCIs, even their reinforced skeletons, meant nothing. The nanos were what kept everything working. It was what healed them. What spoke to their various robotic components so that they worked as a natural extension of themselves. Without them … they were no better than humans.

Chapter Six

Back in a tunnel, with no light and a horny recruit staring at her ass ...

"Would you mind not following so close?" she grumbled. She could practically feel the heat of his grin even if she couldn't see it.

"What's wrong, gorgeous? Feeling *hot*? Turned on by our intimate setting?"

"No, but that sandwich you gave me is making my tummy rumble and not in a good way. If I were you, I'd give myself some breathing room."

The excuse shocked him into laughing. "I can't believe you said that."

"Me either," she grudgingly admitted. "But seriously. Keep a little space in case I run into something, like a pit. I might need you to haul me out."

She was only half kidding. It was pitch-black inside the narrow tunnel, and she could only feel ahead of her, which hampered their speed as she groped the floor of the duct before allowing herself to crawl forward. It seemed like an eternity before gray light filtered in through some kind of vent.

"I see something," she murmured.

"Is this where I tell you to go toward the light? Or should we bypass it in case it's a trick?"

"Tell you what. I'll go where it's not pitch-black, and you keep going. Scream if you find something. Say like rats or a dark hole." As for her, she'd had enough of rubbing her knees raw and second-guessing whether she'd made the right choice. She'd take her chances with what lay beyond the grille.

"Is this your way of saying you're not enjoying our adventure?"

"This isn't an adventure. Or have you forgotten who we work for?"

"All work with no fun makes for a—-"

"Good soldier," she finished. "Now shut up, just in case there's someone up ahead." It was probably too late for stealth, given they'd not exactly been quiet. But, still, she wanted to concentrate on what might possibly await in the light. Hopefully not guns trained on the opening.

While she'd mostly believed him when he said this was probably part of their test, a tiny kernel of doubt also existed and wondered if the test was one of patience that required her keeping her ass sitting in a chair back in the boring white room.

Too late now. Peering through the mesh screen of the barrier over the duct, she noted an empty room. How anticlimactic. The walls were the same pristine white as the one she'd left, but instead of furniture or people, the only items of note were four doors, each a different color.

How odd.

Pushing at the grille with hands dusty from their crawl, it swung away from the opening with nary a squeak. With some inching and squirming and an oops from him as his hand touched a body part he shouldn't have—a grope she enjoyed a tad too much—she managed to get herself to ease out of the opening, legs dangling down first. She dropped to the floor, landing in a crouch, eyes darting around as she searched for movement.

A part of her expected alarms to go off or for troops to come rushing in, guns aimed. Nothing happened.

"Look out below," Seth sang. She dodged out of the way a moment before he landed with a flex of his knees. He grinned at her. "Well, that was fun."

"You obviously don't get out enough."

"Oh lighten up, gorgeous. Admit it, this is kind of exhilarating. Top-secret selection by the brass. A locked room. A concealed way out. Think of this as a quest, a puzzle quest. Solve the riddles, and we win a prize."

"Or get dishonorably discharged."

"Pessimist."

"You're one of those annoying people who sees the glass as half full, aren't you?"

"No, I'm the one who doesn't care and chugs it before asking for more. But enough about my amazing philosophy when it comes to life. What have we here?"

"A room with doors. Yay. And to think I crawled through a dark tunnel for this excitement."

"Alone time with me is always exciting."

She groaned. "Can't you be serious for a minute?"

"Nope." Seth wandered the perimeter of the room, peeking at each portal in turn.

She remained in her spot, arms crossed, watching him. "So, Sherlock, what's our next move?"

"Does your asking mean you've conceded to my superior intellect and abilities?"

"No. But, since you're the one with the bright ideas, I'm sure you have a plan."

Because at this point, Anastasia didn't. Four doors. No signs. And no instructions. Did she choose her favorite color? Was there a pattern? Had she missed a clue somewhere along the way? She worried about making the wrong decision. Thus far, crazy and outspoken or not, Seth seemed to know how to play the game the military had them engaged in. *Sink or swim time*. She'd trusted him up to this point, might as well see if he could take them all the way.

"A plan? Bah. Plans are for the meticulously organized. I think better on the fly. It's one of my better traits."

"Somehow, that's not reassuring."

He just grinned in reply and turned back to his perusal of the space. He mused aloud. "So which door do we pick? Red, for the color of my passion, which throbs for you."

She made a moue of distaste but couldn't help the flutter of her heart.

"Blue for the beauty of your eyes?"

He wouldn't win her over with corny compliments, even if she stored them.

"Green for the envy all the other girls are going to feel when they realize I'm a taken man?"

Taken? By who? Seth had a girlfriend? And yet he flirted with her? "You jerk."

"Why jerk? I believe in fidelity, and I should hope you do too."

"I'm not a cheater, but given your actions with me, apparently you are. What does your girlfriend think of you flirting with other women?"

"I don't know. You tell me."

"Excuse me?"

"Well, I wouldn't have presumed to call you my girlfriend yet, given we haven't even gone out on our first date, but I'm glad to see I'm not the only one feeling the instant attraction. What do you say once we pass this latest test, we go to dinner and then back to my bed in the barracks, or if you'd prefer some privacy, I know of a supply closet."

"I never meant— That is I am not your—" His smile grew wider and wider the more flustered her words emerged. "No."

"Oh come on, gorgeous. Why not?"

"Because."

"My mother always said because wasn't an answer. You'll have to do better than that."

"Fraternizing is against military rules."

"Yes it is, and yet soldiers marry each other all the time."

How had they gone from talking about dinner to marriage? "Why is it so hard for you to accept no for an answer?"

"Determination is my middle name. You might as well give up now. We will get to know each other better, even if I have to coerce you into agreeing." He grinned.

Flattered, she couldn't help a spurt of warmth, but she wasn't about to show it. She growled. "Fine. I'll make you a deal. We'll go to dinner and then your place if you can choose the correct door and get us out of here, alive, and not in trouble, within the next fifteen minutes."

"Hmm. That doesn't give me much time to do my hair."

His what?

Seth finger combed his short locks, straightened his somewhat wrinkled uniform, and then strode to the yellow door, swinging it open. He swept her a bow. "After you."

"What's in there?"

Seth didn't even bother to peek. "Our future life together."

How corny. Yet how true. She just hadn't realized it at the time.

They strode through the door to find the odd balding man standing there with a clipboard.

"Fantastic," he mumbled. "And so much quicker than the others too."

"You mean we passed the test?" she asked.

"With flying colors. Although, in a real situation, less talk might be better. But I'm glad to see a duo emerging. We could use a close-knit pair of the opposite sex in the project."

"Project?" She blinked, trying to process what that could mean and still stunned that Seth had been proven right all along.

"Yes. What did you think these batteries of tests were for other than to select candidates? You're lucky you chose the right partner. Others in your group didn't fare so well."

"What happened to them?"

"Nothing that will cause permanent damage."

She swallowed hard at the nonchalant way the little man said it.

"But who cares about the failures? You two made it through. Although, I do have to ask, Private Murray, what made you decide on the yellow door instead of the others?"

Seth wandered the room, peeking at the various screens flashing images on the wall. He didn't pause in his snooping as he spoke. "Anyone who paid attention would have seen the clues."

Anastasia almost said "What clues?" but, not wanting to appear stupid in front of the civilian, kept her mouth zipped shut.

"Could you elaborate?"

"I noticed the red door bore singe marks around the edges, as if the paint had been exposed to heat. That kind of heat doesn't usually bode well, especially for those of us who like our hair. The blue door exuded extreme cold, even while shut, and being a West Coast boy, I prefer to avoid that kind of chill. The green one smelled funny, and my mother always said to avoid things with bad odors. Which left the yellow door."

"Or the vent," prompted the man with the clipboard.

"Yeah, the vent." Seth shook his head. "No, that wasn't an option. While my partner was bravely sacrificing herself by checking out the room first, I ran a little test. I sent a button I pulled loose rolling along the vent floor. Not hard, just enough to see what might lie ahead. Except it didn't come to a stop, but kept on rolling, and then pinging as if it bounced down a steep slope. Seeing as how I didn't know what was at the bottom, it seemed healthier to take my chances with some doors, especially once recruit Kettle ascertained the room was free of hostiles."

Anastasia could only gape at Seth as he calmly listed his reasoning, none of which would have occurred to her. She also couldn't believe how he'd made it seem as though she'd sacrificed herself on purpose.

"Excellent deductions." The crazy man scribbled happily away, and Seth tossed her a grin. In a murmur for her ears alone, he said "And I always did love yellow."

To think she owed the events that came next to the fact he liked the color of sunshine.

Chapter Seven

Deep in space, still arguing ...

"We need to go back or, at the very least, send Joe and the others a message," Seth demanded as he paced the slim confines of the cockpit.

"No can do," his wife blandly replied. "Or did you want to ruin my groundwork and put a target on your homeworld?"

He froze and spun to pin her with a glare, which she ignored as she studied her console. "Of course I don't want to draw attention to them. But the fact the company has cyborgs in their possession and is torturing them is information they should have."

"And, if they're quick about acting, they'll discover it at those coordinates I gave them."

"Were you always this stubborn and frustrating?" he growled.

"Yes. It's one of my more endearing traits."

Funny how when she threw his own favorite lines back at him they weren't as entertaining. He clenched his fists lest he punch something. For a moment, he could almost sympathize with Aramus. The ornery cyborg constantly lamented how Seth drove him nuts. *I finally understand how he feels.* He didn't enjoy it one bit, but he strove to not let it show.

"What is this super secret plan of yours that requires my help?"

"It's not super secret, just complicated."

"So lay it out for me."

"I can't. Not entirely."

Seth rolled his eyes. "Whatever. Just tell me what I'm supposed to do then."

"I think I found a guy who knows the location of the company head and source for cyborgs."

"You found both? Are you fucking kidding me?"

"You should know I don't joke."

"There was a time you did."

"Things have changed."

"So you keep telling me. Tell me about the guy. Who is he, and where do we find him?"

"He's a scientist, and he's on board the ship we're rendezvousing with."

"So what's the problem? If he's on board, then you obviously can get close to him. Hack his computer files and find out where it is. You have the skills. You don't need me for that."

"Just one problem. The location isn't recorded anywhere. Trust me, I've looked and looked deep. If this guy is aware of the location, then he didn't save it anywhere anybody could find it. My best hypothesis is that it's in his head."

"I get it now. You want me to torture him to get the info? Why not do it yourself? Or have you gotten squeamish again? I thought our missions cured you of that."

"If you're implying I've grown soft, then I would be more than happy to prove you wrong. In very painful detail."

"Ohh, gorgeous, tease me why don't you."

The dirty look she shot him just made him laugh. "Pervert." It was muttered under her breath, but he caught it anyway. His smile widened. "If I thought I could pry it out of him, I would. However, I can't just torture one of the crew without getting caught. And, trust me, I've thought about it. I've run all the possible scenarios for taking him without notice and extracting the intel, but none of them show a viable rate of success. At least not according to the dozen or so simulations my BCI ran."

"Then boyfriend or not, it's time you resorted to an unbuttoned blouse, a wink, and some bow-chica-wow-wow." With a click of his tongue and a roll of his hips, Seth mimed a dirty act, all the while grinning as he waited for her to explode. To his surprise, she didn't get annoyed with his suggestion. On the contrary, a smirk appeared on her face.

"That's exactly the plan I had in mind. Only one problem. Our target isn't into women." She eyed Seth from head to toe, and he had an urge to run as he realized where this was going. "I'll give you one guess as to what I need you for."

"You want me to seduce him?" Um, yeah, that unmanly squeak? It came from him.

"Seduce. Flirt. Shake your tight booty at him until he's ready to spill anything to have an intimate moment with you."

"There's no other way of getting this info?"

"None. Do you really think I'd have gone to find you and risked my cover if there was another way?"

"No," was his disgruntled reply. "Fine. I'll do it. But you'll owe me for this."

"Think again, *husband*." She sneered the word. "Once you get me what I need, I'll give you access to the cloaking technology and dump your ass on the nearest way station."

"While you what? Flit off to tackle the head of the snake on your own?"

"Have you ever known me to flit?"

"No. But I do remember your stubbornness in doing things solo even when having a team or someone as backup would have served you better."

"Why, Seth, are you volunteering to help me?"

Was he? Seeing as how they both had a common goal—finding the origin of the cyborgs and the company and eradicating it—yes. "I always did enjoy a challenge."

"We'll talk more about it once you've gotten the location of the cyborg origin."

Oh, they'd talk more before that, hopefully with fewer words and more tongue. "How long until we meet up with this mother ship of yours?"

"A week or so, give or take a day. It's not like they're sitting still."

A week to try and glean more information. A week alone with the woman of his dreams. A week to convince her to dump her boyfriend, believe him when he told her he'd never done her wrong, and to get her to fall in love with him again.

Piece of cake.

Or not.

Standing from her seat, she stretched before she turned and finally met his gaze. "The autopilot is on, and since there's nothing better to do, I'm going to put myself in stasis mode to recharge my mental and physical batteries."

Put herself in a deep sleep? *Oh no, she's not taking the easy way out and avoiding me.* While some cyborgs swore by long periods of rest to build up extra stores of energy, the truth was most could get away with following a human regime of a few hours of downtime a day. Just like they could go days on end without rest or food. All part of the wonderful world of cybernetics.

Isn't it time you became a cyborg? Eat what you want, when you want. And without gaining an ounce of fat. No need for a toilet. Today's enhanced units recycle all materials to almost 100% efficiency.

With those kind of benefits, why did the military need to force the unsuspecting into the program? Probably because cyborgs were created as cannon fodder for the wars humans started and as guinea pigs to test out the environments of new and hostile planets. Add to that no pay, no vacation, and no playtime, and you have the definition of a slave. It would take something a lot less intelligent than a machine to realize what a raw deal this was. *And the humans wonder why we revolted.*

But back to his wife, who thought she could avoid a long, overdue conversation by putting herself into a coma-like state.

"Sleep? But we have so much to catch up on. Such as, why you never gave me a chance to prove the charges against me were bogus." Instead of trusting him, she'd let her jealousy consume her and refused to listen.

"Prove what? I saw the video."

"A doctored video. You know, there's this thing called splicing and editing. Even kids can do it nowadays with the technology we have. No matter what you think you saw, I never cheated on you."

"Really? Because in case you didn't know, I saw you and heard you with my own two eyes and ears flirting with that Russian slut at the ball the tsar threw. You going to tell me I imagined that too?"

Ah yes, the infamous last dance. He'd been masquerading as a rich playboy, she as an embassy bigwig's arm candy. They'd both flirted and smiled with other people as part of their cover. "I was doing my job. We were spies, remember? Our mission was to ferret out information about nuclear arms and deals by any means possible."

"And we both know you'd do anything to win."

"Kill. Steal. Lie. Even flirt, yes. But I never seduced that woman." Even if he'd awoken in bed naked with her and possessing no recollection of how he'd gotten there.

Of course, she'd bring that salient point up. "If you're so damned innocent, then how did you end up in the sack with her?"

"I was drugged." It was the only explanation. Drugged or the Russian bitch got a hold of one of his programming codes and shut him down. He'd not even known about that kill switch in his neural interface until later. He'd long since gotten rid of it, but he'd often wondered if Natasha, that marriage-wrecking spy, had used it. And, if she had, who gave it to her?

"Drugged?" Anastasia snorted. "Sure you were. By then, we were both swimming in nanos. No way a simply mickey took you out."

"Well, she did something. Drugged me or zapped me or something. Believe it or not, it's the truth. Next thing I knew, I woke in my hotel bed with her on top of me trying to get a little too personal."

"Aha, so you admit being in bed with her."

"Yes. I never denied that. But nothing happened. I told her to get the fuck off. She did and laughed, saying she'd gotten what she wanted. When I demanded she explain, she pointed a gun at me, blew me a kiss, and walked out. I immediately reported what happened to our handler, who told me not to worry about it."

"That doesn't make sense."

"Which part?"

"All of it." Anastasia frowned. "Our handler is the one who told me about it."

"Joel is the one who showed you that damned video?"

"Yes. He also told me it wasn't the first time he'd caught you screwing around on me."

"He did what? That son of a bitch! I'm going to kill him." Slowly and with a lot of pain. Seth was trained in the art of keeping his victims alive for maximum torturous effect.

"Too late. He got taken out in the revolts at the cyborg training camp he was assigned to."

"Pity."

"Yes, because now I have a few more questions for him because he's also the one who gave me the order to hunt you down and execute you."

"Then you won't be surprised to discover he's the one who told me you'd gone rogue and gave me the same order."

"What?" The surprise in her eyes and exclamation was genuine.

"You heard me. I also got the order to execute, wifey poo, except I refused to comply."

"I never heard about that. And you never told me."

"You never gave me a chance."

Her lips flattened into a straight line. "I was angry."

"Say it like it is. You had a jealous temper tantrum."

"I did not."

"Did too. Which in itself was unusual. I mean think about it. You didn't bother to question. Didn't bother to dig. You just accepted what they told you. Then hunted me down and refused to even listen."

The furrow on her brow deepened. "What are you saying?"

"I think it wasn't just normal jealousy and anger at work. I think they used your programming against you."

"No, I would have …" She didn't complete her thought. She whirled and stared at what passed for their window into space. Right now it showed scrolling numbers instead of distant stars. When she did finally speak, her tone was low, almost a whisper.

"You think they tampered with my emotions and thought process?"

"Yes."

"You're accusing them of playing us against each other."

"I am totally telling you they did. I would have proven it to you, too, if you hadn't freaked out and run away. Not your fault. You weren't the only one with hidden bombs in your brain."

"I didn't run. I asked to be reassigned."

"And yet, the girl I knew, the girl I fell in love with would have never run from a fight."

She didn't answer, but her body language spoke for her. Her shoulders slumped, and a weary sigh leaked free. "You said they ordered you to kill me, yet you didn't. Why?"

"For some reason, they either didn't try the same trick with me, or it didn't work. Joel gave me some half-assed story about you flipping to the other side and that I was to kill you if I saw you. I didn't believe a word of it, of course. Before I could ask you about it, you had your jealous meltdown and told me I was a dead man if I didn't leave. So I left, figuring you'd come to your senses."

"But I didn't."

"No. You didn't."

"There's one thing I don't get though. If you knew they fucked you over—"

"Fucked *us* over."

"Whatever. If you knew they did that, then why did you keep working for them? Because I remember how you felt about liars."

"I didn't let on that I knew their charges against you were bogus. I needed an in and access to their intel if I had any hopes of finding you again." He shrugged. "I didn't want to help the bastards, but I knew I wouldn't stand a chance of finding the truth, or you, if I left. So I stayed on in the hopes that I'd eventually locate you and get you to listen to reason, to see past their damned attempts to brainwash. But events conspired against me. Against us. The edicts to exterminate cyborgs came down, and well, we both know how hectic life became. It doesn't mean I didn't harbor a hope that one day I'd get to clear the air with you."

"Is this where you tell me you've loved me this entire time?"

"I did. I still do." He caught her gaze as he made the declaration, willing her to believe him. Hoping for … he wasn't sure what. A sign she still felt the same? No such luck.

The snort was loud and disdainful. "What a crock of shit. Next thing I know, you'll be telling me you haven't slept with any women since our breakup."

"I've slept with women. Just like you've slept with men. I said I had hope, not that I'd become a martyr. You left me, remember? Your love for me wasn't strong enough to see past the web of lies they built, and you walked out. I won't deny that hurt. Still hurts. But we know the truth now. We can work together on building a future, and—"

She held up a hand and stopped him. "Even if what you say is the truth, and much as it galls me to admit it, it makes the most sense, nothing has changed. Too much has happened. I've changed. You've changed. The whole fucking world has changed. Not to mention, I've moved on. Or have you forgotten I'm involved with someone else now?"

He fought back the primal growl that threatened at the reminder. "I remember what you said. The real question is, do you love him?" Seth didn't wait for her reply. He didn't want to hear it. Didn't even want to contemplate Anastasia loving another.

He'd discover the truth the only way he knew how. By touch.

Despite her claim she'd moved on, she didn't even make a token protest when he pulled her into his arms. On the contrary, her lips parted for his kiss, and while she didn't cling to him, neither did she move away. He embraced her with the pent-up passion of a thousand lonely nights. He tried to show her that, despite it all, his fervent desire for her had never abated. By the end of the long kiss, they were both breathless, despite not needing to inhale, and flushed, even though they were capable of regulating their temperature.

"You shouldn't have done that."

"You're my wife." He never tired of saying it. Seth didn't have a possessive bone or machine part in his body, except when it came to her.

"I betrayed you. You should hate me."

"I forgive you." And he did. He couldn't hold her accountable for a decision and emotions forced upon her by outsiders. The military and the company who made the cyborgs were the ones to blame for their past. They'd twisted their love for each other and used it as a weapon to separate them. *To hurt us.* For that, they would pay. *What do you know? Aramus and I finally agree on something.*

"I am sorry. I wish we could rewind time and that I'd realized just what they'd done to me. But I didn't."

"So we start over. I am ready to forget the past and forge a new future."

"It's not that simple. I'm taken."

He snorted. "Oh please. Tell me your new boyfriend can make you lose control of your machine and touch your humanity?"

She didn't answer, but the fact that she refused to meet his eyes said it all.

"I still love you, Anastasia."

"But sometimes," she said, anguish and regret heavy in her tone and eyes, "love isn't enough. Goodnight, Seth. I'll see you at the rendezvous point."

And, with that, she turned on her heel and went into the small cabin that housed a pair of bunks.

It occurred to him he could follow and force her to admit she still cared for him. That he could seduce her body, warm her heart, and have her cry out his name. He could also hack into the autopilot on the ship while she slept and turn it around. Or, given the madness spinning his subroutines into a loop, he could drive their craft into the sun. He could do anything he damned well pleased while she slumbered.

But I won't.

None of those things would change her stubborn mind. Only time would. Time and trust and proximity. He'd managed to seduce her once before with his charm and utter awesomeness. The challenge was, could he do it again?

Damned straight I can because I know deep down inside she still loves me. She just needed time to process what happened and come to the realization that she did.

Patience. Understanding. A moment to reflect. He could give her that. He would give her the world or anything she wanted, starting with his help on this mission. A mission that grew more and more intriguing.

Just what secrets hid in her pretty little head? Exactly whom would they rendezvous with? He couldn't wait to find out.

And he wanted to meet this boyfriend of hers. Actually his fist did. It itched to say hello. His commanding officers always did say he had a problem with impulse control. Some things never changed.

Chapter Eight

Several months after their acceptance into the project, still buried deep underground.

Seth never did get to first base with Anastasia, despite the fact he'd chosen the right door. And it wasn't for lack of trying. Once Dr. Osgoode accepted them as candidates in the project, there was little time for anything but training and testing, followed by more training and testing.

Who knew the human body had so much blood, sweat, and curses to give?

All the recruits participating in the program—a grand total of eight once they'd been weaned down from a starting point of thirty, their initial ten plus others gleaned from other recruiting bases—were housed underground instead of in the barracks. Forget the dorm-style life. They were given separate quarters and locked up tighter than a virgin in a convent guarded by a pack of gun-toting, fervent nuns. Seriously. The only time they got to socialize was at meal times under supervision or on training exercises. Which, given the strenuous nature, left little breath for talking.

In spite of the fact they were treated like well-loved lab rats, Seth had the time of his life.

Seth dropped his ploy of finishing middle of the pack. He didn't have a choice. To ensure he kept up with one taunting blue-eyed temptress, he had to drop his devil-may-care attitude and actually apply himself. To his surprise, he enjoyed indulging in his competitive side. Especially since he'd finally found a worthy opponent. The love of his life, whether she'd admit it or not, was more than up to the task of keeping him on his toes. And shoving him off balance.

For every hurdle he crossed, Anastasia was right alongside him. For every puzzle he solved, Anastasia was seconds before or after him. He'd never met someone with such an ambitious streak, and they fed off each other, leaving the others in their dust. It became a game to see who would finish first. More often than not, they ended in a tie. But the times they didn't ... he laughed as she cursed him and his forebears out. She smirked when she completed a task ahead of him. Their taunts became almost legendary, and Seth caught, more than once, the grudging exchange of money as those watching bet on the outcome. They truly were made a well-matched pair.

Except when it came to bouts of strength.

Seth's bigger size gave him an edge because, unfortunately for her, they went through the same hand-to-hand combat training. Every move she attempted on him, he knew the counter. She threw a punch; he blocked it with ease. He tossed one back, and while she defended well, she couldn't help but grunt or give a little behind his greater mass.

Yet she never cried uncle or gave in. Not Anastasia. Wrestling and sparring, their skill and speed growing the more they practiced, they built up a sweat and incurred many a bruise on the mats.

Their skill was such that they often ended up with a ring of spectators, watching and goading.

But, in the end, when it came down to sheer strength, if he managed to get a grip on her and hold on, Seth won.

And, boy, did it piss her off.

"This is so unfair," she grumbled from her position beneath him, a position he quite liked. However, given they were both sweaty, aching, tired, and wearing clothes, not to mention being ogled by an avid audience, the moment didn't exactly scream romantic.

"Face it, gorgeous. I am your master." Yeah, he totally deserved the jab to his kidney. Excruciating pain or not, he still grinned. "What's wrong? Truth hurt?"

"You're such a jerk." She glared at him.

"Aw, you say the sweetest things. I love you too."

And he did. He loved her intensity and drive. The way she analyzed things and saw past the veneers people used to hide motives and clues. He totally enjoyed the fact that she didn't give in to his charm and made him work for every smile and every stolen kiss. Damn did he love those kisses, rare as they were.

Despite her attraction to him, Anastasia wasn't the kind of girl who just jumped into bed with a guy and had her wicked way. She possessed, as his mother would have called them, morals. It annoyed, even as it charmed the hell out of him. It also made him more determined than ever to make her his.

Now if only the damned military and its project managers would lighten up. Or at least ease their living conditions. *Would it kill them to give in to my many requests to save on costs and make her my roommate?*

Apparently, his letter of recommendation that he share a room and bed with her, thus reducing the amount of cleaning staff hours required for their rooms and the fact that they'd need only one set of sheets, didn't sway his superiors. But he'd not given up. One way or another, he'd find a way to spend some time alone with Anastasia.

It didn't happen the day he pinned her to the mat and rubbed his nose against hers to the laughter of a crowd. As for the next day, Anastasia was missing.

"Where did Recruit Kettle go?" he asked his trainer.

"None of your fucking business," snapped the sergeant in charge of his physical workout. "Now drop and give me two hundred."

"Is Private Kettle okay?" he queried the nurse who took his daily vitals.

"No idea. But I'm feeling a little frisky," she purred with a wink.

Everyone he questioned had no idea where his feisty nemesis and almost lover had gone to. It worried him.

Almost a week passed, a week full of worry and depression. It was with a glum face he entered the gym only to stumble to a halt as he noticed who did stretches on the mat. *She's back.*

His heart stuttered to a halt as he soaked in her appearance. Wherever she'd gone, it hadn't affected her outward appearance. On the contrary, she appeared more vivid than ever. Her skin shone with health, she vibrated with energy, and he couldn't help the surge of lust that roared through him as he eyed her sweet ass in the short gym shorts she sported.

"Gorgeous!" he exclaimed. "I missed you." More than he could have ever expected. How light he felt and happy to see her again, not to mention relieved.

She pivoted with impressive speed and smirked. "Missed me? Ha. You just missed having real competition."

"What can I say? No one can compare to you." He spoke truthfully.

Her eyes sparkled at his compliment. How he wished he could find them a private room with five minutes alone so he could make them smolder instead.

"Feel like working off some excess energy?" She tossed the challenge at him with a coy smile.

"Depends, are you taking off your clothes?"

A husky laugh escaped her. "Tell you what, if you can pin me to the mat, I'll let you get to second base during lunch."

"Only second base?"

"Second and maybe I'll let you sneak into third," she added with a lick of her lips.

Now there was a contest he wanted to win. Piece of cake. "Prepare to have yourself fondled," he announced. Apparently, she'd missed him, too, because they both knew she couldn't pin him. It seemed absence made the heart grow fonder or her body horny enough to take things to a new level. Whatever the cause for her change of mind, he'd take it.

For some reason, she felt a need to talk when they engaged, exchanging lazy shots easily blocked as they warmed up. "Did you know there are several more levels below this one?" she said in a conversational tone as she jabbed him with a left hook, pouring on the speed despite them just starting out.

Oho. She wanted to play rough, did she, and distract him? Ha. As if that would work. Seth could take a few shots for the team. In the end, he'd run the bases.

"Yeah. This place is massive. One of the guards let slip that there's actually fifteen floors, although he didn't see all of them. Apparently the elevator only goes to level ten. Anything past that requires special clearance."

"Because that's where they keep the really top secret stuff." She swept her foot, so fast he stumbled as he leapt over it.

"Are you implying you've seen these levels?"

"Seen," she admitted with a left hook that grazed his jaw and sent his head snapping. "Stayed for a while." She followed up with a knee he caught barely with his thigh. "And experienced."

That final word caused him to freeze, and he didn't counter the sweep of her foot that took him down to the mat. "What do you mean experienced?" he asked from his prone position. He rolled before she could land atop him and sprang to his feet.

"Watch and see."

If he'd thought her faster than usual before, now things got ridiculous. Seth could barely get his arms in position to block the rapid-fire flurry of punches and kicks aimed his way. And fuck, did they hurt. Each impact drew a grunt. A gasp. A silent "holy shit!"

It was as if his sweet Anastasia possessed super strength and speed.

As if she'd been … enhanced. The revelation paralyzed him, and he couldn't stop himself from toppling to the ground. Nor could he stop the little dynamo from leaping atop him and pinning him. And when he said pinned, he meant it. She held him with her same little hands and lithe body, but with a strength greater than his own.

"Aha!" she crowed. "Gotcha!"

Elation shone on her face, but Seth could only whisper, "What have they done to you?"

"Say hello to the new and improved me," she announced, rolling off him. She stood and offered him a hand. He didn't exert himself at all as she pulled him up. He didn't have to. She yanked him to his feet all on her own.

"You let them experiment on you?" he asked as he mopped his sweating—and yes, bruised—face with the towel kept in a stack by the locker room door.

She shrugged. "Not so much experiment as improve."

"Improve how?"

"I'm not supposed to tell."

He frowned. "Did they hurt you? Threaten you?" The thought they might have coerced her angered him, not that he could do much about it. As a simple soldier, he had no say or power to do anything. But an impotence when it came to protecting didn't mean he didn't want to know.

Taking a long pull from a bottle of water, she paused before answering. "No one twisted my arm if that's what you're asking. Dr. Osgoode simply asked me if I'd be willing to try something that would give me an edge."

"Did he mention if this edge came with danger or side effects?"

"Yeah, jealous recruits who can't handle the fact they got their ass handed to them by a girl."

"I'm not jealous."

"Then why can't you act happy for me? For once, I'm not the one getting her butt plastered to the mat. Now, even though you're bigger, I don't have to concede. If I lose, it will be because my skills are lacking not because I don't have a Y chromosome or a piece of meat hanging between my legs."

"Hey, watch what you call my man parts. You'll hurt Arthur's feelings."

"Arthur? What the hell kind of name is that for a penis?"

"It's a mighty name. A name fit for a king."

She shook her head. "Only you would name your dick."

"Oh please, like you don't have a pet name for your girl bits?"

"It's called a vagina."

Seth recoiled and placed a finger on his lips. "Shhh!"

"What do you mean shhh?"

"Don't ever use that word to describe nirvana."

"Why ever not?"

"Because it makes me think of my seventh grade biology teacher and the semester we spent studying the human body. That man took a perfectly good word for a beautiful body part and turned it into something that makes me shudder when spoken aloud."

"Vagina." She smirked. He winced. "V-a-g-i-n-a." She drew it out, smiling all the while.

"You're an evil woman, Anastasia."

"I know. And do you want to know how evil?"

"How?"

She leaned in closer, her lips near enough to flutter warm breath across his. "So evil that I'm now going to laugh about the fact you lost the bet. No second base for you."

With that taunt, a wink, and a swing of her perfect hips, she sauntered away.

Leaving him more in love than ever. And determined.

Chapter Nine

Back aboard a ship with a woman determined to ignore him ...

With Anastasia supposedly recharging her batteries, Seth plotted. Somehow he doubted she slept as she claimed. He knew he wouldn't, not knowing what she was capable of. *Like she'd leave the biggest, baddest spy she knows without supervision. Not likely.* But he didn't call her out on her cowardly hiding. Not yet. First, he had some other tasks to take care of, tasks well suited to one of his training. He did what he did best, ferreted out information.

Seating himself in the control seat for the craft, he hooked himself to the onboard computer and sifted through the various files. Well, his BCI did. Seth, however, pondered other things—the fact he'd not bathed or changed since disembarking from his last mission. Hard to seduce when wearing boring, comfy space clothes that had seen better days. He mulled over the fact that Anastasia alluded to knowing the location of other cyborgs, cyborgs in possible trouble. This truly didn't sit well with him. For one, Seth wasn't one to idly stand by when others needed his aid. And, secondly, he didn't like keeping secrets. He kept too many already. As an intelligence model, known in his military files as SO101 (Anastasia being SO100), he was predisposed to keeping information confidential. One of his biggest covert cover-ups was how much he remembered. Pretty much everything.

He could recall, in living color, his youth from the years he'd excelled in school and played football to his graduation with a sobbing mother and a beaming father. He recalled the car accident that killed them both, leaving him orphaned in college and with no funds once the estate was settled and the government took its cut. With few choices, he'd enrolled in the military, a sure way to an education, a job, and a future.

He'd learned combat skills. Met the love of his life. Got trained physically and mentally to become an expert in information gathering—and assassination. Once he was transformed into a cyborg, his training continued, faster than before. He could remember each painful step. Each exhilarating accomplishment. The adrenaline of his first mission. The betrayal of his lover and his employer.

Other than the shady spot in his memory surrounding his creation as a cyborg, he never forgot a single thing. Except how to tell the truth. Was it any wonder Anastasia accused him of lying about Natasha?

The irony of the fiasco, though, was that incident was probably one of the few times he was not in complete control. Much like the boy who'd cried wolf, when he claimed innocence, no one, or should he say the person who most mattered, believed him.

If I weren't so logically minded, I'd blame karma. But Seth knew better. He knew who'd engineered the failure of his marriage. The military, which according to the ships logs, was exactly who they were going to rendezvous with in six days, thirteen hours, and seven minutes.

What. The. Fuck. He'd foolishly trusted Anastasia, and she'd betrayed him. They weren't just going to join a research crew. They were meeting up with a company research crew under direct command of the military.

"Anastasia!" He bellowed her name, not at all surprised she didn't reply. He'd spent hours submerged in his thoughts and the computer system. Hours sifting through bogus logs, many detailing, in glaring, boring detail, his homeworld planet—sans the cyborgs population, one thing she'd not misled him on. However, covering up their existence didn't forgive what he discovered after. It took a lot more digging to decipher their route and the mother ship they were supposed to rendezvous with. It was less mother ship and more like battle cruiser.

Just what was Anastasia up to? *Is she planning to hand me over? Plotting to commandeer the vessel? Are we going on the undercover mission of a lifetime?*

Only one way to find out.

Striding through the small craft, it took only a few moments to reach the cramped room that contained only compact bunks. His wife lay on the bottom one, eyes shut, hands folded across her stomach, the perfect image of a woman in repose.

How lovely and innocent she looked. A true prince charming would lean over and kiss those soft lips. A loving husband would spoon her to keep her warm.

Not Seth. He yanked on the blanket beneath her and dumped her on the floor.

Amidst her thrashing arms and legs, she yelled, "What is your problem?"

"My problem, dear wife, is you lied to me."

"About what?" she asked as she untangled herself. She flipped her hair back and peered at him from her sprawled position on the floor.

"Not going to deny you're a liar?"

"Nope. At this point, there isn't much in my life that's based on the truth. The question is, which part are you objecting to?"

"You lied to me about who we're going to meet."

"Not lied so much as didn't exactly tell."

"You're splitting fucking hairs."

"I hope not. I paid a lot for my conditioner."

"Not funny."

"Says the guy who used to use that line on me on a weekly basis."

He growled. "You're working for the military. That's who we're going to meet."

"I see someone went snooping. You managed to get past my firewalls quicker than expected."

"You knew I'd find out?"

She rolled her eyes. "Like duh. You wouldn't be a very good spy if you didn't take a peek. I expected you to check up on me. It's what I would have done."

The fact that she didn't even deny his accusation raised his ire a notch. "Well, since you're in a truthful mood now, then care to explain what you need me for? What am I? A present? A bribe? A rat for them to experiment on?"

"Calm down before you get your panties in a giant knot."

"As you well know, I don't wear underpants. I prefer to go commando." His reminder had her gaze flicking to the area in question, and it irritated him to no end when his cock responded with a wakeful twitch. *Oh no way. She is not going to distract me with sex. Not this time.* "Did you happen to mention that to them, *traitor?*"

"I can explain."

"Really? Because I'm trying hard to think of a reason you wouldn't have told me before. I mean, you came to me asking for help, fed me some bullshit story about working for some research group, and yet, all along, you were in cahoots with the enemy. How could you, Anastasia? I trusted you when you said my people weren't in danger."

"And they're not."

"Please forgive me when I say I don't believe you. Pretending to be an undercover operative for the company is one thing, but actively working for the military too? That's crossing the line. Which is why I sent a warning to Joe."

"You did what?"

How dare she appear so indignant? "Ears not working? I said I warned the cyborgs back home."

"You should have spoken to me first."

"Why? So you could lie some more? My primary concern is keeping my fellow cyborgs safe."

"They were safe. Why do you think I went through so much trouble creating a cover story for them?"

"I don't know. Maybe to try and fool me into thinking you were working for the greater good."

"I am."

"Says the woman who kidnapped me and is en route to meet with the enemy."

"Our enemy."

"Says you."

"When did you become so paranoid? What happened to the Seth who always saw the silver lining?"

"He got betrayed one time too many by the people he trusted."

She didn't quite flinch, but he caught the subtle change in her expression. Apparently, she didn't like it when the accusation was aimed at her.

"I can't believe you sent a message," she grumbled as she picked herself up off the floor. From a shelf where she'd left them folded, she yanked on some cargo pants and a T-shirt over her athletic undergarments before stalking out. He followed at her heels.

"You left me no choice."

"What part of you'll ruin the plan did you not grasp?" she snapped.

"First off, don't you dare play the part of betrayed damsel. I had to. Joe and the others need to know our planet might be compromised. There's not just cyborgs on the surface. We've got women and children in that compound. Lame humans too, humans the government dumped into unsustainable colonies." She stopped, and he ran into her, but he didn't allow the impact of their bodies to distract him.

"They're alive, not dead?"

"Of course they are."

"I wondered about those rumors."

"Don't tell me you believed the false media reports that claimed we slaughtered them all or used them for parts?" He sneered. "We are cyborgs, not unfeeling animals."

"I never believed the rumors, but you wouldn't believe the number of folks who do."

"I never underestimate the stupidity of others. Especially since I am apparently the king of idiots for believing you."

"Oh stop with the melodrama. Despite what you found, it's not what it seems."

"So you're going to tell me you don't work for the enemy?"

She continued toward the control room of the ship. "Oh, I do work for them. But they don't know what I am."

"How can they not know you're cyborg?"

She turned, probably so she could better sneer at him. "Just because your subterfuge and ability to blend is rusty doesn't mean my skill to fit in has suffered the same fate. I've spent years perfecting this cover. I've worked my way through the system, hiding my cyber roots at every turn, infiltrating the military as well as the company at the deepest level."

"For what purpose? Because we've already ascertained you're not saving cyborgs in need."

"I've saved those I could without revealing myself."

"How convenient for you. But deadly for them."

"Don't judge me. I've had to make some harsh decisions to get where I am."

"And where is that?"

"Only steps away from discovering the location of the cyborg source as well as the head of the company."

Whatever scathing retort he'd planned evaporated. "You've found the source of our nanos?"

Many believed that cyborgs were simply humans with machine parts. And they were, in a sense. Many of their less effective organs were replaced with metal ones run by sophisticated microelectronics and nanotechnology. What most didn't realize was the nanotechnology, the teeny tiny foreign bots that circulated in their blood, were what made them truly special. Without the nanotech, cyborgs would be little better than humans. They'd heal at the same rate. Age and die like a human. Eat, drink, and, in general, be a human, just one with an ability to set off metal detectors.

What made them more than men was their nanos, and the source of those nanos was the biggest secret of all. Even Joe and the others who'd recovered their memories didn't remember much about how they became cyborgs. As far as Seth knew, he and possibly Anastasia, the first two spy models who got to keep their minds and memories, were the only two who bore faint recollections of their rebirth. Faint because the military did their best to wipe them.

"I know many might not understand the reasoning of my choices. Sometimes I wonder myself. All I know is since the order came down to destroy us, maybe even before that, I've been looking for the man who started the project. The one who made the decision to inject us with unproven DNA and technology. I wanted to …" She trailed off.

"What? Kill him? Thank him? Ask him for more?"

She bit her lower lip and turned from him. As if he'd let her hide now. He grasped her by the upper arm and forced her to face him. "Answer me. What is your objective?"

"I want to ask him why."

Chapter Ten

A long time ago, after kicking the ass of the boy she liked and then taunting him …

It irked Anastasia to no end when Seth disappeared after their conversation and match. For once she'd won.

Or is that lost?

Despite the elation that she'd finally managed to best him in a test of strength, Anastasia couldn't help but wonder if she'd truly won when it meant the prize he'd meant to claim—a kiss and more—ended up not to be forthcoming.

Perhaps I should have given him a consolation prize. One they could have both enjoyed. Playing hard to get wasn't just frustrating for Seth. It pained Anastasia as well.

Never in her twenty-odd years had she faced such an urge to throw caution to the wind and to forsake her goals for the fleeting pleasure that came from indulging in attraction. Then again, never before had such temptation tried to sway her.

What began as a contest of wits, skill, and training had somehow evolved over the past few weeks. Sure, Anastasia engaged Seth in a battle to see who would end up on top, but more than that, she'd come to like the rascally blond with the ready smile and wicked humor. No matter what the military or the company in charge of the program threw at them, Seth replied with fervor, a grin, and a joke. Even the rare times he didn't finish first, he was gracious, not like other men, or even women for that matter, that she'd known, who liked to rub the loser's face in their success. Unlike her.

Taunting him is probably the highlight of my day. While being with him was what kept her going.

If it weren't for Seth, Anastasia might have flaked out of the intense program a while ago. Sure, she enjoyed the challenge, but she couldn't help but wonder at the purpose. *What exactly are they grooming us for?* She feared she wouldn't like the answer.

Squashing her qualms, she focused all her energy toward succeeding and finishing on top. She loved seeing the shine in Seth's eyes as they pitted themselves against each other, although she had a feeling their one-on-one matches were drawing to a close. More and more, those in charge paired them, turning many of their exercises into partner sessions. They were a couple in training, learning to work and fight in tandem. To her surprise, she rather enjoyed it. She knew she could count on Seth to have her back. That kind of trust in someone was new, but welcome.

So welcome that Anastasia now yearned for something more than just a joining of their skills. *I wouldn't mind a chance to join our bodies.* Or at least do something about the desire he could incur with just one wink and a mischievous grin.

Of course all that was before she'd gotten her upgrade. Anastasia wasn't just a soldier in training anymore. Actually, she had to wonder how human she was, given what flowed through her nervous system. In her defense, the way Dr. Osgoode had termed it when he pulled her aside and proposed it to her made it seem like the simplest of procedures. No worse than taking a vitamin to improve her physical health. And he convinced her by playing on one of her weaknesses—pride.

"I see Private Murray has bested you once again in the gym."

"Yes, sir. Sorry, sir. I'll try harder next time." What else could she say at his obvious reference of her failure to beat Seth time and time again.

"Don't be sorry, recruit. It's not your fault you were born female. Weaker than your male counterparts. Forever destined to be on the bottom."

"Thanks." Not. Nothing like rubbing her face in it. If she wouldn't face a court marshaling, she'd have liked to rub her fist in the jerky doctor's face.

"What if it didn't have to be that way? What if you had the strength to beat him?"

"I don't understand."

"We can give you something to make you stronger."

"I don't do steroids." Not with their dangerous side effects.

The doctor's brows raised as his face took on an astonished expression. "Steroids? Good god, no. Nothing so pedestrian. I'm talking about the way of the future. A way to make all humans better versions of themselves via the use of science."

"I'm afraid I don't understand sir."

"Nanotechnology and cybernetics, my dear girl."

She wrinkled her nose. "You mean like robot parts and tiny computers?"

"If we're to use simple terms, then yes."

"I thought that was still years away from being feasible."

"Or so the general public thinks. What if I were to tell you that the future is already here? That a select group of people, perfect specimens such as yourself, are being groomed to be the first to receive the gift of enhancement?"

They could kick her ass out if they didn't like her answer, but Anastasia wasn't about to become a science experiment. "I'd say no thank you. I'm not a guinea pig."

"Again, you misunderstand. We're not talking possibility. We've done it. Those who've received the gift no longer need doctors. They can heal themselves. They are stronger, faster, smarter … Why, the wonders are never ending."

"So you've gotten some of these enhancements."

"Alas, no. The person controlling the project has been very picky about who can receive the gift. They believe only the very best should be considered candidates. And you are one of the chosen few."

"Me?"

"Yes, you. You've proven your intelligence, your strength, and your loyalty to your fellow man and your country. What better candidate than someone with your exemplary skills and attributes?"

Who wouldn't feel flattered at that kind of praise? Still, though, she wasn't about to blindly accept. "What are the side effects?"

"None really. We simply inject you with the nanos, and they go to work, healing cells, accelerating your regular bodily processes."

It seemed too easy. "But they're machines."

"Not in the sense you're thinking of. For one, they are beyond microscopic. Undetectable by all but the most sophisticated equipment."

"How do they work?"

"I'm afraid that is confidential, but suffice it to say, they don't require outside intervention to function. Nor do they burn out or change your current physical and mental makeup."

"So what you're saying is I would still be me."

"Of course. Just a stronger version of you."

A stronger version? Oh, the temptation. "Could I beat Seth?"

"You could beat any normal man."

"How much time do I have to think about it?"

"Until the end of this conversation. Understand, there are only limited spots available. We're offering it to you first, but if you're unsure, then there are plenty of other candidates who would jump at the chance. I, for one, wish I could receive the treatment."

The wistful tone in his words said it all. Yes or no? Take a chance or pass it up? Go big or go home. "What do I have to do?"

It turned out the process was simple. But excruciating.

Just remembering the pain as the staff filtered her regular blood out to allow the new blood a chance to enter her body and circulate made her shudder. *Simple injection my ass.* Funny how she could remember the agony of the process but little else. She vaguely recalled a bright light, shining in her eyes. The sterile smell that only hospitals seemed to have. The murmur of voices, but not the words. Pain overshadowed everything else.

But other than that, she couldn't deny the results. Dr. Osgoode spoke the truth. She was stronger. Faster. And she could heal in a way she would term as miraculous, although discovering that ability was a shock. In her defense, she dared anyone to volunteer to let a stranger, even if he did wear a white coat, slash them with a knife. She'd snapped and called the orderly who dared to cut her a nasty name while holding him in a headlock and threatening to kill him until she noted the inch-long gash he'd given her had healed over in minutes.

Awesome. *I'm like an impervious superwoman now.* Yet, best of all, despite the little bot things running around her body, she still felt like herself. The mirror reflected back her face, albeit without the scar by her left eyebrow where she'd gotten stitches when she was sixteen after falling off her bike.

Say hello to the new Anastasia. Of course, she couldn't wait to use her new abilities on Seth, to see if, for once, she could gain the upper hand in hand-to-hand combat. She won! But with guilt piquing her, she'd admitted to him that she'd changed. Apparently he couldn't handle it, because she'd not seen him since.

With Seth missing, and the doctor not making his usual rounds, she had to wonder if Seth had finally lost interest, or had her partner also been chosen to undergo the same treatment.

Was he, at this very moment, screaming? Did he, too, wonder what lay beyond the drawn curtain through which the rubber tubing carrying the nano-infected blood came?

The best question of all, though, was what did the company and military want of them now that they'd begun to transform the recruits? It didn't escape her that the training they'd undergone was more than basic military training.

A grunt in the field of battle didn't need to know one hundred and one ways to kill a man barehanded. A simple soldier didn't require lessons on etiquette and fine dining or how to open locked doors.

If this were the CIA, I'd say they were grooming us to be spies.

As it turned out, the CIA was a cover to hide where the true espionage happened. But Anastasia didn't discover that until later.

It took only five days to her seven for Seth to return, and she immediately noted the change in him. For one, while he still sported the same jovial grin, there were lines bracketing his mouth, lines of pain that had yet to ease.

When she entered the gym on the sixth day of his disappearance, she froze when she noticed him already there working out. Despite facing away from her, he seemed to sense her arrival and he turned his head, his eyes immediately searching her out. "Hello, gorgeous," he said as he stretched on the mat, his athletic body bending and twisting.

She couldn't help but watch his every move, mesmerized by the power his muscles promised, aroused by his very maleness. It seemed absence made the body fonder.

"Hey, I was beginning to wonder if you'd quit."

"And miss out on all the fun and great food?" His sarcasm didn't have its usual levity.

"You all right?" she queried.

"Never better. You are looking at the new and improved Seth."

"So you visited the levels beneath us?" she asked as she joined him in warming up.

"If you mean did I get adapted, then yes." His lips thinned.

"You don't seem too happy about it."

"I wasn't given much choice."

She paused in her stretching. "Did they force you?" Because, while she hadn't exactly dove into the procedure one hundred percent certain, she'd made the choice, like it or not.

"Not exactly."

"Then what?"

"It doesn't matter."

He spun away from her and headed to a treadmill, for once ignoring her. She didn't like it one bit. Positioning his back to her, he set the machine to a quick pace and pumped his legs to keep up with the whirring rubber mat under his feet.

Disturbed at his out-of-the-norm behavior, she stalked after him and slammed the button on the console, sending the running machine to a halt. "Talk to me, Seth. What happened? Why do you seem so upset?"

He wouldn't meet her eyes. "It's no big deal. I'll get over it."

"Your body language says otherwise."

"You think you know me so well?"

In some respects, yes. Enough to guess he'd not gotten the nanotechnology willingly. "Despite our rivalry, I'd like to think we're friends. Talk to me."

At first he seemed determined not to reply, but she wouldn't walk away, not when she felt as if he hid something important from her.

It took almost a minute of silence before he gave in. "Anyone ever tell you that you're stubborn?"

"As a mule."

His lips curved in a ghost of a smile. "One of your best qualities."

"Along with my great legs."

"I would have said ass, but, sure, those work too."

"You're stalling. Spit out what's bothering you."

A moment passed as if he fought an inner battle. "I did it for you."

He said it so softly that she wondered if she heard him right. "You what?"

"I said I did it for you. When I realized what they intended, I got cold feet. I asked for time to think about it. More information. But they made my choices crystal clear. Either I took those nano things into my body then and there, or they were going to kick me out."

She wrinkled her nose. "If you didn't want them, then why did you agree? Why say it was because of me?"

"Because I didn't want to leave the program." His gaze rose and caught hers. "I didn't want to leave you. So if my choice was to become super robot man capable of keeping up with a gorgeous robo chick or living a mundane life alone?" He shrugged and his lips partially lifted, a wan smile that caused a stutter in her heart. "I chose you."

If she'd wondered before, the way her heart stuttered to a stop answered for her. *Oh my god, I think I'm in love.*

"Oh, Seth." She reached up and touched his cheek, cupping it. He angled his face into the simple embrace, and his eyes closed.

"You probably think I'm an idiot. I mean, who gets weird shit injected in them to impress and keep a girl?"

"A guy who deserves better than me."

His eyes flashed open. "Funny you say that because I keep feeling like I need to do more to deserve you."

"Idiot."

"Not according to my IQ tests."

Trust him to turn a serious conversation into a joke. It eased the tension though and she laughed. "What am I going to do with you?"

"Hopefully naughty, naked things. Hey, do you think they'd let us have some alone time so we could do some testing of our own?"

"Making out isn't testing."

"It is if you're trying to see if this shit they put in us makes us last longer and recuperate faster in the bedroom."

How could one naughty wink heat her from head to toe?

Before she could reply, their drill sergeant entered the training room and began barking. As Anastasia went through the motions of exercise, she couldn't help but replay Seth's words, over and over. *I did it for you.* What did that mean? Was it a declaration that what he felt for her went beyond mere flirting?

A flutter of her heart hoped that answer was yes.

Chapter Eleven

Back to the future.

Three days into their voyage found Seth no closer to winning Anastasia over. Considering the smallness of the vessel, it should have proven difficult for her to avoid him. But she managed it somehow.

When she wasn't recharging her batteries in the cyborg version of sleep, she was plugged into the computer, eyes closed, face blank, sifting through the missives and information that came through her newsfeed channels.

But Seth didn't like to be ignored. Just ask Aramus or any of his cyborg brothers. He needed daily contact, whether physical or mental. Her pretending he didn't exist wasn't working for him, not when he couldn't stop himself from thinking about her, recalling all they'd gone through. Pretending they had a future together. Imagining her naked and flushed beneath his heaving body.

Oh no, she wasn't going to rid herself of him so easily. *I have ways of making myself seen and heard.* And he employed them. With nothing better to do, and determined to get some kind of reaction from her, Seth entertained himself by driving her nuts, a specialty of his.

On the first day she tried to ignore him, he played with the computer. She cursed him out soundly once she discovered he'd reprogrammed the onboard computer voice from a generic male one to a sultry female one who enjoyed using naughty adjectives and imbued every query with a sexual undertone.

"Hello, captain. How may I *serve* you?" purred the computer from the embedded speakers.

Seeking him out, a glower on her face, Anastasia growled. "What did you do?"

"Whatever do you mean, dearest wife?"

"Don't play dumb. What did you do to the computer?"

"Oh that?" He smiled. "I was bored. So I made some changes."

"By turning our ship computer into a phone-sex kitten?"

"I know. Pretty awesome, don't you think? It took me a few hours of downloads and splicing, but I'm rather pleased with the overall effect."

An effect that ranged beyond his perverse pleasure into snarky enjoyment as he got to watch Anastasia grit her teeth every time the computer spoke aloud.

But after that short confrontation, she once again deigned to pretend he didn't exist.

Day two, he did his best to get in her way. Every time she went to move, he happened to get in her path. She reached for a tool to tweak a component on the console, his hand was there accidentally brushing hers. She went to use the tight hall to go from the control room to the cabin, he happened to be there, too, going in the opposite direction, his body rubbing against hers as they slid by in the tight space. She went to sleep in the bunk and woke to him snuggling her, an arm and leg thrown over her body.

"What are you doing?"

"I'd say it's obvious what I'm doing. Getting some shuteye."

"In my bed."

"Our bed."

"You do know there's a top bunk."

"Not anymore, I needed the mattress for something."

That something saw him pitching it from an airlock into space.

"This isn't going to work," she growled as she shoved at his limbs, which he stubbornly refused to move. Good luck. Enhanced or not, she wasn't budging him unless he decided to move.

"What won't work? Sleeping together? Why ever not? We used to do it all the time. Usually naked. But, out of deference to your boyfriend, I kept my bottoms on."

"This isn't right."

"You're right. I'll get chafed if I remain dressed. I'll take my pants off."

"You will not!"

"Testy, testy. Someone needs her beauty sleep."

"Someone needs to stop driving me insane. If this is your lame attempt to get us back together, it's failing miserably. I already told you I'm not interested. I have a man in my life."

He adopted a feigned expression of innocence. "You think I'm trying to seduce you?

Perish the thought. The idea never crossed my mind."

"Liar."

"If you ask me, I'm not the one who can't keep my mind out of the gutter. Here I was, just trying to get some shuteye, and you're turning this into a big deal. It's not my fault you can't handle the sight and feel of my awesome body. I realize I'm irresistible, but, really, learn some control."

"I am not tempted."

He bit back a smile at her indignation, and the lie that his processor spotted. "Sure you're not. You can touch if you want. I won't get offended or tattle on you to your boyfriend."

For his generous offer, he got a knee to the groin, a shove that sent him tumbling to the floor, and a foot in the gut as she used him as a stepping-stone on her path to escape him.

He grinned. His plan to get under her skin was working marvelously.

Day three, he did laundry. But did Anastasia appreciate it? Of course not.

"Where are my clothes?" she bellowed as she woke from her nap. Having just exited the shower, his timing intentional, Seth grinned as he stood underneath the air dryer. In space, towels were considered a waste of space and resources. Why bother when a hot air dryer could do the same thing and not end up on the floor in a sodden heap?

Thus, it was, with only a smile and nothing else, he greeted his wife when she stormed into the small bathing chamber.

"What have you done with my clothes?"

"They're in the wash," he announced, lifting his face into the warm air and letting it evaporate the moisture still clinging to his skin.

"All of them?"

"Yeah. Funny thing happened. While I was getting dressed, I happened to spill my morning breakfast shake all over our stuff." Cramped quarters meant little in way of storage. Apparel for them both shared a large drawer out in the hall. "Somehow I didn't think you'd appreciate the wet stains, so I threw the entire drawer into the wash, and I even picked up the stuff you'd dumped on the floor."

"So what am I supposed to wear in the meantime?"

Turning, he eyed her up and down, lingering on the valley between her breasts covered by a generic sports bra then dipping lower to admire the indent of her waist, the slightly defined muscles of her stomach, and finally to the hip-hugging shorts she wore. "If you ask me, you're wearing too much as it is."

She crossed her arms over chest. Silly woman. Didn't she know that just made her even more alluring?

"I'm getting tired of your games."

"Who says I'm playing?"

"I am not going to sleep with you."

"As if you'd have time to sleep," he scoffed.

"You're impossible."

"I prefer the term do-able."

"Do yourself."

"I tried. My five fingers just aren't enough. I want the real thing. I want my wife." He said the last bit in an utterly serious tone. Some things he didn't joke about, and his need for her was one of them, and she knew it. He could tell how his words affected her by the way her eyes glazed and her breathing stuttered. She'd always worn the marks of passion so well, and she could never hide them. From him at least.

"I'm going back to bed," she snapped.

"Good idea."

"Alone."

That's what she thought. She whirled on her heel and stalked out, but he followed close behind. Despite her claim, she bypassed the rumpled bunk and headed out to the hall, probably to check into the main control area or the status of their laundry.

Perhaps now wasn't the time to remember that he'd forgotten to push the start button to get the load going.

Regulating his core temperature so he couldn't feel the chillier air of the ship on his bare skin, he trailed her.

Flopping into her command seat, she shot him an evil stare, or tried to. Apparently it slipped her mind that, once sitting, she'd put herself eye level with something that was proving, in a very visual fashion, how happy it was to see her.

Where he failed to hold her gaze, his cock snagged it. "Would you cover that thing?" she muttered in a husky voice.

"With what? All my stuff is in the wash."

"Then wrap a sheet around yourself or something."

"Why? Is the sight of nakedness bothering you? It shouldn't. We are, after all, part machine, capable of controlling both our bodily functions and emotions."

"If you're so capable, then why do you have an erection?"

"Because I, unlike someone I know, choose not to hide what I feel."

She didn't reply, but she did manage to turn away and fiddle idly with the buttons on her console.

Seth wouldn't let her ignore him though. Not this time. Gripping the armrests to her chair, he spun it, forcing her to face him. She kept her gaze averted.

"When are you going to admit you want me still?"

He expected her to deny it again. But Anastasia always did have a knack for surprising him. "Will you stop harassing me if I admit a part of me still desires you?"

Why do a mental fist pump when he could do a real one? "Hell yeah!" he exclaimed, giving a double air pump. "She still wants me. She thinks I'm sexy," he sang.

"She also thinks you're annoying."

"But that hasn't stopped you from picturing me and you in carnal positions."

"Unfortunately, it hasn't."

Okay, so her tone and expression didn't exactly scream, "*I'm so in love with you!*" Still, Seth considered it a step in the right direction. Much as she might try and deny it, she felt something for him. And it was more than just irritation.

"What do you propose we do about it? I know I'm willing to let you have your debauched way with me."

He expected a slap or punch to the gut for his outspokenness. He knew he skated on thin ice with his over-the-top attempt at flirtation, but, in his defense, he didn't know what else to do. A declaration of undying love would probably send her bolting. Diving on her without express permission could see him seriously harmed. And walking away? Yeah, that wasn't an option.

What he didn't expect was for her to give in so easily. "If we have sex, will you stop this insane campaign of yours to get under my skin?"

"If we have sex, I will do anything you want."

"Including doing what I say when we reach the mother ship?"

"Sure." And he meant it, for the moment. As an intelligence model, he possessed the prerogative to change his mind as conditions changed or new intel was gathered.

"This doesn't mean our marriage is back on," she warned as he leaned down to seal the deal with a kiss.

"So it's all right if I pretend I'm cheating on my wife with someone else's wife?" he murmured against her lips.

"If it turns you on."

Everything about her turned him on, especially the challenge she still posed. Yes, she might have conceded the war when it came to lust, but the battle for her heart still required waging.

But now, how to proceed?

He still stood in all his naked glory. She still sat, partially dressed, perusing him with an amused tilt of her lips and a challenge in her eyes.

I can't screw this up. Which meant he needed to make this about her. Simple enough.

He dropped to his knees, a supplicant to the woman who owned him heart, body, and metal.

She regarded him from under eyelids grown heavy, a sure sign of arousal. "I've dreamed of this moment," he admitted, skimming his hands up her thighs, the skin as smooth as he recalled, the hitch of her breath still just as a tantalizing, even after all this time.

He bent his head to trace his lips along the same path his hand took, lightly brushing her skin, inhaling the scent of her. Her legs parted before his subtle caresses, an unspoken permission that he could proceed.

And he would. At his own sweet pace.

He blew hot air against the seam of her shorts, loving how she couldn't control the impatient wiggle of her bottom or the musky scent of her arousal as her sweet honey pooled.

Placing his mouth upon the thin fabric, he blew again, warm moist air, which caused her to gasp and grab at his hair.

"Stop teasing," she moaned.

"But teasing is what I do best." But how could he have forgotten that, in that respect, she always beat him? Down skimmed her hand, over the tautness of her belly to the waistband of her bottoms. In slipped her questing fingers, and no matter how many parts the military replaced, no matter how much of his body his BCI controlled, it never could stem his desire for this woman or the fact that a simple act such as her touching herself could still make him drool.

Watching the subtle motion of her hand under the fabric was more than he could bear. With brute strength, he grasped the fabric of her shorts and tore, shredding the flimsy barrier and allowing him a perfect view of her pussy. As if he hadn't just found visual heaven, he also got to see what naughtiness her fingers were up to.

Beneath his avid gaze, she spread her slick folds, pink temping flesh that he longed to taste. She slid in one digit then two, pumping slowly, in and out, an erotic tease and reminder of what his cock would soon enjoy. The scent of her musky arousal enveloped him, a decadent perfume never replicated by any other, one whose delightful scent had the ability to make him tremble—and his cock to engorge even more painfully than before. He could have shut off some of his receptors to prolong the moment, to help him through the suffering, but he chose to feel every nuance of the seduction. For so long, he'd existed in a vacuum, playing the part of a human so well that his cyborg brethren often wanted to beat him to a pulp. But, in truth, until this very moment, until Anastasia re-entered his life, he'd but pretended at life, pretended at humanity. Now, with his body afire, his nerves singing, all his senses open and experiencing, he felt ... *alive*.

As a third finger joined the first two, Seth couldn't help but groan. When it came to titillation, he was but a pupil to his mistress, his wife. As if his inadvertent sound were a signal, Anastasia withdrew her fingers out of her wet sex and ran the damp fingers in circles over her clit.

He'd denied himself long enough. He went in for a taste. A lick. A dive into nirvana. Her honey flavor exploded on his tongue as he lapped at her sweet sex. He delighted in exploring every inch of her pussy, dipping his tongue into the moistness of her channel, flicking it over her clit, which her fingers abandoned to grab hold of his hair instead. Her hips rocked in the chair, a silent yet telling motion that told of her enjoyment. He couldn't help but hum his approval against her, a vibration that drew forth a cry from his sweet wife.

And his name, uttered on a soft sigh. "Oh, Seth."

How he loved her. He did his best to show her with the worship of his mouth and tongue on her body. He ignored his own needs as he brought her to the pinnacle of pleasure then toppled her over it, the strident cry as her orgasm washing over her the most beautiful thing he'd heard in a long time.

But he didn't stop there. Anastasia had always been a responsive lover capable of more than just one climax. He knew from experience that the first was just a precursor to the more powerful second. So he kept on lapping at her, his motion concentrating more intently on her clit, that sensitive nub that he caught with his lips and teased.

"Seth." She groaned his name, the need in the tone letting him know it was time. But her position in the chair wasn't conducive for what he had planned. He grabbed her around the waist and lifted her, placing her bared ass on the humming smooth spot between the control panels that manned the ship. He spread her legs and inserted himself between them, nudging her sex with the tip of his cock.

"Be careful you don't send us into a star," he teased as her hands scrambled at her side for purchase.

She forewent looking for a stationary handhold and grabbed hold of him instead. He sucked in a breath. "How about instead of you worrying about my steering, you make me see stars?" she replied in a husky voice.

She'd see the Milky Way if she didn't stop what she was doing, using him like an erotic toy, rubbing his swollen head against her wet sex.

Removing her hands from his cock, he held them overhead and forced her to lean back, and then he slid into her. By all the nanos in his body, no pleasure in the galaxy could compare to the heat and tightness of his wife.

In he slid. Out. Each thrust a jolt to his synapses. Each suction of her pussy an exercise in control. Faster he pumped, increasing the friction, multiplying the pleasure. He released her hands to hold her around the waist, steadying her for his thrusts. Deeper he slammed. Harder. Quicker. She got tighter. Wetter. More vocal. Their breathing turned ragged despite their modified systems. Their skin flushed, at odds with their usual temperature control. Their bodies exploded, unable to stem the ecstasy that overtook them both.

As he held her trembling body in his arms, the only thought that coherently formed was, *How could I have ever let her walk away?* The answer was simple. He wouldn't have. *I didn't. They* made him. *And I can promise right now, it won't happen again.* He'd wage a war, by himself if need be, to hold onto the woman in his arms – although he was pretty certain Aramus and a few others would back him if he went on a rampage just for shits and giggles. He'd battle for her heart. Fight to regain what he'd lost. Nothing would keep them apart.

Except for maybe her stubbornness, which he'd have to work on. No time like the present while she was still soft and malleable.

Stroking her hair while nuzzling her temple, he murmured, "Do you remember the first time we slept together?"

"How could I forget?" she replied wryly. "It was our very first mission together. You told me that we had to have sex to make our cover believable."

"And was I right?"

"Well, I'm still not convinced we needed to have that much sex."

He growled, and she giggled. "But it certainly didn't hurt. On the contrary ..." She tickled her fingers down his back before giving his ass a squeeze. "It felt damned good."

Good? Ha. It had been explosive. Fantastic. The whole mission was a success from their first time together to their first kill.

"I've never forgotten that day," he admitted. Because it shaped their future.

Chapter Twelve

Back to the past and the meeting that changed their lives ...

Their first time together came about because of a mission. Actually, it had happened during the mission.

A few weeks after receiving the nano injections—and after hours of intense training to test the new limits of their bodies—they got called in front of their commanding officer, but he wasn't alone.

Anastasia clacked her heels and executed a crisp salute, a move aped by Seth, because before them stood a man with stars and bars, lots of them. Only an idiot didn't show proper respect to a general, especially one with a cold, piercing gaze that said he'd have no problem demoting their asses and have them shoveling out latrines.

"At ease, soldiers." The gravelly tone went well with the steel-wire hair brushed with gray, the hard lines on the general's face, and his no-nonsense demeanor. If the creases in the commanding officer's uniform had been any sharper, they would have sliced to the bone. Here was a man made for the military life. *Here is a man you don't want to piss off.*

Seth took an instant dislike to him. Something about the rigid general set his inner warning bells ringing, and for some reason, he itched to wipe the callous expression off his face. As it turned out, had he given in to his first impulse and just killed the general, he might have saved himself a whole lot of trouble later on. Actually, he would have probably saved a whole lot of cyborgs.

But, at the time, he was still a good little soldier. So when General Boulder told him and Anastasia to stand down, he told himself to relax. The guy was military after all, which meant he had rules to follow, rules that no one told Seth General Boulder made up as he went.

"Your CO tells me you're the best pair of operatives he's got."

"Our CO is a smart man, sir," Seth replied. Disagreeing at this stage of the game seemed inadvisable.

"I have my doubts about that, which is why we're going to put the two of you to the test. We just received intelligence reports informing us that a big arms deal is about to go down. I want you to stop it."

"You want us to infiltrate their operation, sir?" Anastasia asked.

How cute and naïve she still was. Seth read the situation a little better. "You want us to kill someone."

A cruel smile pulled the general's lips taut. "We prefer the term problem solve, and it's more than one person. We want the heads of the two negotiating factions taken out. With leadership of the opposing factions in disarray, it will void the deal and cause enough chaos to keep those groups from planning anything further in the near future."

"You're sending us in as assassins?" Anastasia gasped, her face ashen.

"Assassins kill for money," the general snapped. "You are military personnel. You follow orders for the good of your country to save lives, which makes you undercover operatives with a mission."

Chastened, Anastasia's lips thinned into tight line, and she nodded. "Yes, sir."

Yeah, he could call it what he wanted, but what the general demanded still smacked of assassination. Not that Seth bothered to argue. In this situation, it would accomplish nothing but antagonize the rude bastard. Seth, not liking the rebuke any more than her—*because call it what you will, we're still being asked to kill*—tried to defuse the tense atmosphere with questions. "How are we to accomplish this, sir?" Poisoning? Sniper bullet? Hand-to-hand battle? Heck, Seth could already picture them getting air dropped and parachuting into a compound at night, dressed in the latest camouflage gear. Boy was he wrong.

"You'll be attending a gala event hosted by one of the negotiating parties. It's one of his wives' birthdays or something. You'll be attending as a rich American couple, a usually reclusive one, whose cover we've been building for a few years. You," the general fixed Seth with a hard stare, "will be the son of the billionaire, and she will be your wife. You'll be briefed on the details during the flight over. Succeed and this will be the start of a brilliant career. Fail and …"

Funny how the lack of a punishment sounded more ominous.

"We won't fail, sir."

"You'd better not. We've spent a lot of money and time making you into what you are. Failure is not an option. Now get going. Dismissed."

Anastasia held her tongue until they hit the hall and were out of earshot. Then she grabbed his arm and hissed. "What the fuck was that about? Yes, sir. We won't fail you, sir," she aped in a high-pitched voice. "Kiss much ass lately?"

"The guy's a pompous jerk. So, yes, I kissed ass a bit. Pissing him off wasn't going to benefit us."

"But agreeing to be killers is? He's asking us to kill in cold blood. I didn't sign on for that."

"First off, you heard him. We're not killers but undercover operatives."

"With a mandate to kill."

Her insistence on clinging to ideals that never existed irritated him. "What else did you expect? We joined the military. Casualties are a part of being a soldier."

"It's one thing to kill on the field of battle, another to do it in cold, calculated blood."

"Even if it saves millions of lives? How is killing one, two, or more enemy soldiers on the field of battle any better than targeting one or two guys who, if taken out of the picture, means that battle won't ever happen? That hundreds, maybe thousands, of lives will be saved?"

She recoiled from him, her eyes flashing with distress. "I can't believe you're agreeing with this."

"I never said I did, but I understand the logic and can see the benefit. I also know, in case it's slipped your mind, that we don't really have much of a choice. We are soldiers. Special soldiers. You can't tell me you didn't have an inkling this was coming."

"I wondered." Oh, how grudgingly she admitted it.

"And now it's time to put our training to the test. If you ask me, it sounds a lot more exciting than getting tossed into a trench with a bunch of other grunts forced to eat military rations and camping. Not to mention, I'd prefer to not end up as cannon fodder for guys with stripes who plan their strategy from the safety of their guarded headquarters."

"So I should be excited I'm about to be an assassin for my country?"

"Yes. What else can we do but turn it into an adventure? We will be the Mr. and Mrs. Smith of the military. We will go on this mission. Play the part of rich snobs. Eat fine food. Wear ridiculously expensive name-brand clothing and save thousands of people from the follies of two power-hungry asshats."

"When you put it like that, it sounds almost fun."

"Because it will be." If one ignored the fact he'd have to kill his first and second human being. But he couldn't dwell on that. He needed to focus on something more positive, such as the fact that, from the sounds of it, their ruse might need to last for a few days. And hadn't the general claimed their cover was that of a married couple? Couples got to share a room—and a bed.

Him plus Anastasia, alone with a mattress made for sinning? He'd kill a heck of a lot more than two scumbags to live out that fantasy.

Chapter Thirteen

On an airplane en route to her first mission for the military, and her first kill.

Despite her trepidation over the mission, Anastasia had to hand it to the general, he and the ones piloting this scheme hadn't spared any expense when it came to keeping their cover intact. From the private jet owned by the fake weapons corporation to the clothing and gadgets she and Seth were outfitted with, everything was top-notch quality.

It made slipping into the role of rich trophy wife and the son of an arms dealer that much easier. Even if Seth seemed determined to treat everything like a game.

Kicking back in casual linen trousers, his white shirt partially unbuttoned, his tie askew, and dangling a half-full champagne glass, Seth appeared the epitome of rich playboy. "Relax, gorgeous. Pour yourself a drink."

She shook her head. "No thanks. I'd prefer to remain clear headed for our mission."

One of his brows arched. "Wrong answer. I think it's time we went over the ground rules again. Or have you forgotten what our trainer taught? Rule number one, once you go in, you need to be in character. That means no more talking about you know what. We'll soon be landing, and we have no idea where the eyes and ears of the enemy might be. Two, if we're going to pull this off, you need to unwind. Right now you look like you're about ready to jump out of your skin."

"Because I'm nervous." And scared. This wasn't a training exercise. If they messed up, they wouldn't get reamed out by their CO or made to run laps. One misstep or wrong word and they could end up the recipient of a bullet to the head or worse.

"Which is why you need to sit down beside me and have glass of wine. Relax your frazzled nerves."

"Easy for you to say."

"You think I'm not freaked out?" Seth asked in a high pitch. "I am, I'm just better at not showing it. Confidence is half the battle when it comes to subterfuge."

"What's the other half?"

"Luck."

When she gaped at him, he chuckled. "Okay, the other half is good planning with a heavy dollop of luck and a prayer that everything works out the way we've planned. Besides, it's too late to back out now. One way or another, we're going to get this done. Whether we're successful or not totally depends on us. So, come on, sit down, and pretend we're actually a rich couple on our way to a fabulous weekend of wining, dining, and debauchery."

"Debauchery?"

A sexy grin lifted the corner of his lips. "If I'm lucky." He patted the seat beside him and waggled his brows. When he did that, it was hard to take him seriously. Look at him trying to allay her worries and fears. Curse him for being so darned adorable.

Perhaps Seth was right—perish the thought and mark it on the calendar as a first. Maybe she did need to stop overthinking and just go with the flow. Plopping herself on the buttery leather loveseat beside him, she snagged his glass and took a large swig.

Then laughed. "You jerk. This isn't wine at all."

"Okay. You caught me. It's apple juice. I was always more of a beer and hard spirits kind of guy. Not to mention, I sometimes get airsick."

"You're not going to throw up, are you?" She shot him a worried look, and he grinned.

"Not this time. Looks like the scars on my buttocks from the buckshot isn't the only thing those nanobots cured me of."

"You were shot in the ass?"

"Yeah."

"I'm almost afraid to ask. Why?"

"In a nutshell? Angry daddy. Not-so-innocent daughter. And me, running bare-assed through a corn field."

She giggled and tried to cover it, but the small chuckle grew and grew until she was full-out laughing.

"Hey, I'll have you know it was anything but funny at the time."

"If you say so," she said, still chortling.

"Brat."

She took another swig of apple juice, twirling the glass between her fingers after she did. "I dare say, *dahling*, this is a delectable vintage."

"Only the best for you, gorgeous."

"What other surprises do you have in store for me?"

"Less a surprise than a promise."

"A promise of what?"

"You do realize we'll be sharing a room."

It had occurred to her, and then she'd tried to forget it. The idea of being in such intimate proximity with Seth did wild things to her body. It made her pulse race, her nipples tighten, and her sex moisten. "Are you implying what I think you are?"

"Was I being too subtle? Sorry. Let me make myself clearer. You. Me. Bed. Naked. Fucking."

Crude? Very, yet there was that fluttery feeling again, the one that made her breathless and flushed her body with heat, lusty heat and desire. "But our mission—"

"Requires us to play the part of a couple. Couples have sex. Think of it as a necessary pleasure to make our cover story seem more believable."

"Even in the privacy of our chamber?"

"Especially in there. And, never forget that once we leave this plane all of our words and actions will be examined."

"You mean you think they might be watching our room?" How could he even think of indulging in sex if someone was keeping an eye?

"Don't tell me an audience freaks you out." The sultry look in his eye told her it didn't bother him one bit. On the contrary, she'd wager it turned him on.

"It's just I—"

"You know what, you talk too much," he muttered before drawing her into his arms and plastering his lips over hers. Forget arguing. He had a point. And she let him make it until the pilot reminded them minutes later—too quickly for them to get more than a few dozen hungry licks and nibbles in—that they would be landing in just a few moments.

Brushing his thumb over her swollen, well-kissed lower lip, Seth murmured, "We'll continue this tonight, *wife*."

She couldn't help but shiver at the promise. Thankfully she didn't have time to mull his words, or worry, because they hit the tarmac of the private landing strip, and the charade of their lives began.

Playing the role of vapid trophy wife was easier than expected. She hung onto Seth's arm and laughed at lame jokes, even those made at her expense. She smiled at him whenever he said something witty. And flushed with heat every time he whispered in her ear, *"I can't wait to peel you out of that dress and kiss every inch of your gorgeous body"*. Funny, because she couldn't wait to get him out of his clothes. Seth dressed in a black tie was a treat no woman could resist. Add to that his casual caresses as he led her around, chatting up their hosts, and his promising smiles, was it any wonder she spent the evening in a dreamy daze. If it weren't for the fact their directive was to kill their host and one of the other guests, it would have seemed like a pleasant, almost fantasy-like vacation.

As it was, their room exceeded the glamour of anything she could have ever afforded. Entering the sumptuous suite, she couldn't help but run her hand along the silky fabric of the comforter, the richness of the cloth unlike anything she'd ever touched.

"Did you have a pleasant evening, dearest?" Seth asked.

Turning to face him, she caught him pulling off his black tie. He tossed it onto a gilded chair. Off came his jacket, also to land in a heap on the fancy seat. His fingers went to the buttons on his crisp white shirt. One loop. Two. She swallowed. A few times. *Is it me, or is it hot in here?*

Off came the shirt, revealing Seth's smooth, muscled chest, a chest she'd seen hundreds of times before during training and sparring. Heck, she'd punched and kicked those abs many a time. What made it different now was that they weren't trying to outdo each other. For the first time, they were alone—if one discounted any possible cameras watching. It made all the difference because now she saw his body as a playground for fantasy and play. And, boy, did she want to play.

He kicked off his shoes and padded over to her, his socked feet sinking into the plush rug. She stood there, frozen and uncertain what she should do.

A chuckle rumbled from him. "Tired, darling?" He stopped before her and, with a finger, tilted her chin up so her eyes could meet his. "And yet, the night has just begun."

His hands, capable of such strength and violence, gently slid the straps of her gown off her shoulders, baring them. He leaned his head and kissed the exposed skin, the soft brush of his breath, the bristly shadow covering his jaw, abrading her skin. She shivered.

"Shouldn't we rest to be in fine form for tomorrow's activities?" Anyone watching would assume she meant the planned excursion to watch a polo match. In reality, she referred to their mission.

Seth brushed her concern aside. "Our presence isn't required until after lunch. Plenty of time to recover."

Any thought of protesting died with his kiss. Gently, he pressed his mouth to hers, softly, and yet the urgency and fire coursing through her was anything but tame. Wild. Desperate. Needful.

The kiss went from a gentle exploration to fierce assault, probably because her hands clutched at him, the nails digging into his skin as she sought to draw him closer to her, to feel the hardness of his body blending with hers.

Her dress ended up in a rumpled heap around her ankles, leaving her clad in only a strapless bra and panties. Neither of the flimsy lace accoutrements lasted more than a moment at his hands. Scraps went flying, and then she felt herself falling back until she hit the silky comforter with a small bounce.

Seth shed his pants before joining her, his heavier body covering hers, the hot, hard length of his cock, trapped between them. Their mouths met in a clash of teeth and tongue as they hungrily devoured each other. There was no holding back now. No one, nothing to stop them.

The weeks and months of sensual teasing, the inability to do more than simple petting caught up, and they both reacted savagely, passionately in the quest to finally consummate the lust they'd denied for so long. She threaded her fingers in his short blond hair while her tongue curled and stroked along his.

The tip of his cock nudged at the apex of her legs, begging for entrance, but she wasn't quite done with him yet. He wasn't the only one who'd dreamed of this moment. Who'd fantasized.

"Lie on your back," she said between panting breaths and sensual tugs at his lips.

She didn't have to ask twice. In between one heartbeat and the next, she straddled him, and oh how she reveled in the position of dominance. To be the one in control. Over him. Over the moment.

Down she slid the length of his body, ignoring his gasped, "What are you doing?"

As if she'd tell him. Let him guess. Let him anticipate. Her hands skimmed his thighs, fingertips dancing on his skin as she went after her prize. Scooping him, she cupped his heavy sac and kneaded it, a sly smile curving his lips as his head went back and his eyes closed.

The perfect image of a man enjoying a moment of bliss. But she was planning more than just a massage of his balls. Forward she leaned, the ends of her hair brushing his skin as her mouth latched onto the tip of his shaft. His hips bucked, but she held on as she licked him, tasting the saltiness of his excitement.

Bathing his cock with her tongue, she explored the length of him, from the mushroom cap down the edged rib then back up again. She swirled her tongue. He cried out. She took him into her mouth and sucked, hard enough to hollow her cheeks, hard enough that he bucked again, hard enough that he pulsed and almost came in her mouth.

The thickness of his cock excited her. The thought of it, all of it, sinking into her, stretching her, *oh god*. She couldn't help but shudder, and her pussy trembled, wet and ready to take him, a fantasy she might have to forget if she didn't stop sucking him.

With a final lick, she released his shaft and straddled him. The swollen head of his cock poked at her damp cleft. Forget further teasing. She sat down.

This time, she was the one to cry out. The hands she'd braced on his chest dug into his skin, and her head went back far enough the tips of her hair tickled her spine. Impaled on his thick length, she didn't move but spent a moment enjoying the feel of him inside her, how he stretched her and filled her so completely. His cock pulsed inside her, a little twitch that sent a pleasurable jolt and spurred her into motion. Back and forth she rocked, pushing him deep, squeezing him tight, meshing their bodies so close that an observer would have been hard-pressed to know where one began and the other ended.

Her orgasm hovered, that tightness inside waiting to explode. As the pleasure consumed her, she lost her rhythm and whimpered.

So close. So close. Oh please.

Seth took over, flipping her onto her back to continue what she'd begun, driving into her with a rhythmic intensity that had her panting and clawing at his back. Just when Anastasia thought she might die if she didn't come, he grabbed her roughly about the hips and changed the angle of his penetration.

Dear heaven. Each thrust, each jab of his thick cock, hit her G-spot after that and threw her over the edge. She came with a scream, her sex pulsing wildly around his pumping shaft. But he didn't stop. Oh no. Even as she quivered and shuddered, he continued to thrust into her, driving his shaft into her over and over until she came again, an orgasm so intense that she opened her mouth to scream but nothing came out.

Everything went into that orgasm. Her voice. Her mind. Her heart. And probably her soul.

And then, only after he'd claimed her, every inch that she could give, did he finally come.

After such a cataclysmic event, everything else on that mission paled in comparison. Playing nice with drug lords, arms dealers, and other rich pricks who thought money ruled the world? Piece of cake.

Being with Seth, really *being* with him, imbued her with an extra layer of ease and confidence. She played her part of wife to perfection. Or so he claimed later when he took her from behind while tugging at her hair, her dress thrown up around her waist.

She stepped into her role of spy without a hitch, overhearing and recalling later for their debriefing the many facts she'd learned as a brainless wife in the company of men who didn't watch what they said.

And when it came to killing? It just required a little pressure on the trigger of her revolver fitted with a silencer. The dread she'd feared? Non-existent. As a matter of fact, when she sneaked into the primary target's rooms while Seth took care of the guards outside, she'd wondered if she'd have the guts to accomplish the task. The whimpers of the young maid as she bore the lashing of a whip wielded by a power-hungry pig made it easy.

Anastasia was more than just a girl in the military now. She was an enhanced cybernetic soldier—and she was in love.

Chapter Fourteen

Back to the future, in time for the rendezvous with the military craft and the next phase of her operation.

"So that's the ship?" Seth leaned over the back of her seat and gazed over her head at the large vessel they approached.

"Yes."

"I don't suppose we have time for a quickie?"

Insatiable man. Since her capitulation a few days ago, they'd spent most of their time in bed having sex. Actually, that wasn't true. The bed wasn't the only place they'd christened. Practically no bare wall, chair, or space hadn't seen them doing things that would make a human woman blush. It seemed they'd both harbored a lusty need for contact. More than contact, satisfaction.

Anastasia had forgotten the ecstasy of a lover's touch until Seth reminded her. With each caress, stroke, kiss, and orgasm, she recalled the other reasons why she'd become so addicted to him so long ago. Like a drug, he entered her system and made her crave more and more.

He was a dangerous distraction she could ill afford. But he was also the only person she could count on to help her.

If he could play his role, which she reminded him for the umpteenth time. "Now, remember, once we land, no more touching and kissing and wife comments."

"I know. I am John Tweed, openly homosexual male whose last partner ditched him before he went on his scientific exploratory mission." He recited his role in between nibbles to the nape of her neck.

"Right."

"What about sneakies?"

"Sneak what?"

"Sneakies, like kids do in college, where boys visit girls rooms in the middle of the night to get some."

"There are cameras and microphones in many of the common areas, the labs, and some corridors, so no."

"I'm really starting to dislike this plan. Once I get the intel, I demand we come up with a new cover for the next phase. One that sees us pairing up again."

She whirled in her seat. "I thought I made myself clear that we weren't a couple. We had sex."

"Lots of sex."

"And sex doesn't mean this marriage is back on again."

"If you say so." A sly smile hovered on his lips.

"Seth, I mean it."

"Sure you do."

She could tell he didn't believe her. Hell, she didn't believe herself. The last few days had been wonderful. If one could forget the crap they'd gone through, she could almost pretend that everything would work out fine. That they'd complete their self-imposed mission and head off into the sunset, once again a happy married couple, in sync on the job, during their relaxing time, and in bed.

But the reality was that kind of walk-into-the-sunset dream wasn't for the likes of them.

"I don't have time for this argument," she growled as she whirled back around to face her console. "Don't make me regret finding you."

"You can count on me. You can always count on me."

She didn't doubt the sincerity of his words. The problem was, revenge had been her focus for so long, could the same be said of her?

The time to ponder would have to wait as she went through the manual steps to dock with the larger ship. Humans couldn't use their brains to interface and multi task. Nope. Playing the role of mundane human meant doing everything by hand. But at least it kept her busy instead of wondering what to do with Seth.

Despite her claims to Seth that no one suspected her cyborg heritage, as she disembarked her small explorer craft into the bigger bay of the military vessel she'd rendezvoused with, she couldn't help but feel a tingle of fear, something her machine side never quite managed to dispel. *Will this be the time I get caught? Have they finally seen through my ruse? Have I led Seth into a trap?*

To her relief, a cadre of soldiers with amped-up Tasers didn't await. A silent sigh let loose in her head and not via her mouth. So far so good. No ugly waiting committee. No one trying to take a swipe at her head in an attempt to decapitate, the only one hundred percent sure way of killing a cyborg.

However, to her dismay, she wasn't exactly home free. Her human boyfriend awaited.

She feigned delight and waved while Seth muttered at her back, "Are you fucking kidding me? That's who you chose as your partner?"

Okay, so Jerry wasn't exactly the most imposing fellow around. Skinny, tall, and not the most athletic of guys, she'd chosen him because he was such a non-threat. He also happened to hold the title of scientist in charge of research and development of ways to disable and modify cybernetic organisms. The irony that the man in charge of trying to eradicate her kind was dating one didn't escape her.

She ignored Seth's snicker and waved. "Hi, darling."

"You're back. Finally," Jerry said, beaming from ear to ear. He wrapped her in a clumsy hug and planted a sloppy kiss on her cheek. Unbeknownst to Seth, hugs and a few kisses were all they'd exchanged thus far, despite her assertions to the contrary. She'd told her boyfriend it was because they worked together and she didn't want to get in trouble. Jerry, being the kind of guy who respected rules, abided by her decision. She dreaded the day when they finally got some planet-side leave though. At that point she'd run out of excuses and would either have to break up or put out. *I could also kill him. Benign appearing or not, Jerry's got a dangerously clever mind.*

"How were things while I was gone?" she asked, linking her arm through his and pasting a fake smile of welcome on her lips.

"Boring. Our latest testing failed. But it seems Denson's crew might have had some success. Apparently we're going to head back to that godforsaken planet now that all the explorer vessels have made it back. What about you? How was your trip? I see you returned with a passenger." Jerry directed his gaze to Seth, who loomed behind her doing who knew what. She wouldn't put it past him to make a gagging face or hold fingers behind her head as bunny ears.

"Meet John Tweed. Only survivor of an explorer vessel that went down on planet HD85512b. Or, as I nicknamed it, planet Blah. What an ugly place."

"Tell me about it," Seth chimed in, his voice adopting a nasally twang. "Why I swear, if I had to eat one more squirmy tree root, I would have died."

"You don't seem malnourished," Jerry observed. "Are you sure this place is such a write-off? We could use some new food sources, especially for the colonies, so we don't deplete the earth's stores."

Shoot. She'd have to remember Jerry's eye for detail. She quickly covered. "Even if you could convince people to get past the taste and look, it doesn't matter. Mr. Tweed here observed indigenous life forms that are intelligent enough to place the planet under automatic protected status from the federation."

"Are you sure of your findings, Mr. Tweed?"

"Call me John." Seth held out his hand, and Jerry reluctantly withdrew his arm from around Anastasia to shake it. "And, yes, I am very sure. I observed them using simple tools in their everyday tasks and also discovered they had progressed from cave dwelling to the building of structures to shelter themselves. Whilst I didn't manage to crack their language, there is no mistaking their ability to communicate."

"Sounds like they've barely escaped from the mud. The general will want to hear about this place before you send in your report."

Of course he would because if no one knew about the creatures then he could wipe them out and claim the planet was open for farming and colonization. It wouldn't be the first time.

Anastasia pretended chagrin. "Oh dear. I didn't think of that. I already filed my findings with the bureau for intelligent extraterrestrial life as well as the one for protected planetary status."

For a moment, Jerry's genial appearance hardened, and his lips tightened, and during that split second, she actually questioned her ability to read people, as Jerry appeared anything but benign. It lasted only as long as a blink before his usual smile took over. "Ah well. I guess we'll have to skip this one and hope the next planet we find has resources we can use."

"Or take," Seth muttered under his breath.

A jab from her elbow kept Seth from making other remarks, but she thought she heard him growl as she tucked her hand in Jerry's crooked arm and followed him down the spaceship's gangplank to the docking bay floor.

"So tell me what's been going on while I was away." As Jerry related a series of boring events, she kept her eyes peeled for trouble. It seemed odd now that she thought about it that only Jerry had greeted her. A soldier or a liaison at the very least should have also been on hand, if only to debrief and take care of her guest.

She interrupted Jerry during some dull tale of his work to ask, "Where is everyone? I would have thought Lancomb or Helger would have shown up by now to take Mr. Tweed here to some quarters and to debrief him."

"The higher-ups are in a bit of a tizzy. Seems we lost yet another female unit to the other side. B785 was reactivated and is now in the possession of the rebel cyborgs."

And he chose to relate news of no import instead of telling her? "Oh dear. That makes three now they've recovered. How are the cyborgs doing it?"

Jerry shrugged. "Appears to be dumb luck, but the project managers are freaking and tightening security around the ones remaining in custody."

Seth just couldn't keep his mouth shut. With a twang so nasal she wanted to jab a pick in her ear, he said, in a tone most shocked, "Do you mean to say you have murdering robots in your possession? I thought they were supposed to be killed on sight."

"The kill order still stands, but given their dangerous nature, and the casualties we incur when taking down just one, it was thought best if we kept some to experiment on."

"I hope you don't have any on board," John/Seth exclaimed.

"A few, but you needn't worry about them. We keep them closely guarded."

John/Seth clutched at his chest with a dramatic gasp. "Aren't you afraid they'll escape and take over the ship?"

"We have fail safes already in place for such eventualities. In the case of an incident, the vessel is programmed to self-destruct."

"But what of the crew?"

Jerry's lips twisted. "Apparently, the lives of a few are considered a small price to pay for the knowledge we might glean. It's why all testing is done either on a spaceship or on remote planets. But enough talk about those murdering bots. You won't be seeing any during your stay. Testing is done under heavy guard and only authorized personnel are allowed near them."

"Are you one of them?"

Jerry's chest puffed out. "I am. It is my belief we need to better understand them if we are to effectively stop them. Or reform them."

Make slaves of us again you mean. How Anastasia wished the time were ripe enough to kill those who still wanted to make tools of the cyborgs. However, the fleeting pleasure of bending Jerry's arms backward until they cracked and he screamed wouldn't solve the larger problem. *I need to know who is behind the project. I need to find the source, or we risk seeing more humans experimented on, more unsuspecting souls changed and tortured for the so-called greater good of humanity.*

Casting a glance back at Seth, she wondered what he thought of the news. On board the ship, when he'd heard about the captive cyber units, he'd lost his temper, quite the feat considering his usual calm demeanor. To her surprise, she didn't see anger or disgust at Jerry's words. On the contrary, he smiled and winked at her.

Then the idiot sent her a wireless message, straight to her BCI. *The only person reforming me is my wife, hopefully with handcuffs and thigh-high boots.*

Despite her urge to kill him, she couldn't help but picture it. And she added a blindfold and scented oil to the scenario.

Not that they'd likely live long enough to act it out, not given his stupidity in using their wireless communication ability. It was her fault for not specifying beforehand that they needed to maintain absolute BCI silence.

Then again, he should have known.

Before they'd made it too far on the ship, Jerry's arm emitted a beep. He peeked down at his communicator and sighed. "Looks like the lab needs me. Much as I'd like to continue our reunion, I need to go."

"I'll see you later?"

"Of course." Jerry placed a sloppy kiss on her lips, and she held herself still lest she shudder.

Seth stiffened beside her.

"What about our passenger?" she asked, inclining her head in Seth's direction.

"There's an empty cabin up the hall from yours. Stick him in there for now. I'm sure the officers will want to talk to him once they stop freaking out."

With another attempt at a kiss, again aimed at her lips, which she managed to narrowly avoid by turning her head, Jerry shambled off. She waited until he was out of sight before rounding on Seth. "Are you a fucking idiot?" she asked through gritted teeth.

"No, but your boyfriend is."

"Don't change the subject. What were you thinking sending me a mind message? We're on a military ship. What in the galaxy possessed you to do something so foolish? You do realize they could have intercepted it, right? We could, at this very moment, have a squad of soldiers preparing to take us out."

"We're fine."

"Fine?" She ogled him. "And just what makes you think that, smart guy?"

"Because the moment we stepped on board, my BCI downloaded a program onto their mainframe that causes it to ignore and not register any cyborg frequencies. We can talk all we like in our heads, gorgeous. Although, I'd prefer to talk in bed."

"I hate you." She walked away from him, sensing without looking that he followed—and watched her ass.

Does this mean I'm not getting anything for our anniversary? he asked, switching to wireless talk.

If you get us killed because of your cockiness, I will haunt your afterlife.

So, unlike the religious groups, you think we have a soul?

I think there's something more out there. Whether it's god, heaven, hell, or even fucking limbo, I don't know. But I refuse to believe we evaporate into nothing. What do you believe?

I think it's cute that after all you've seen and experienced you can still put faith in something with no proof.

Once upon a time, people believed aliens visited our planet, even though we never caught or met a live one.

And people still do.

But now, we know for sure.

WHAT?

Smiling to herself, she didn't reply but stopped before a control panel alongside a door numbered sixty-nine. How appropriate. She slapped her hand on it, and when it demanded a passcode, she entered it. The door no sooner slid open than Seth hustled her in with a growled, "Explain."

"Explain what?"

"Your comment about we know for sure. Last I heard, while we'd found some primitive life, none had yet evolutionized past the basics. You imply otherwise."

"I am not implying. I am stating. We found intelligent life. As a matter of fact, we've got a specimen on board at this moment in cryogenics. We have more on the planet we're heading to. Or did. They're not easy to keep alive so I hear."

"What do they look like?"

"I couldn't tell you. While I know they exist, everything about them is a closely guarded secret. I've been unable to locate images or concrete reports. What I have gleaned, though, is they're vaguely humanoid, with possibly gray skin, spiny ridges down their back, claws, and a bad attitude.

Then again the attitude might have to do with their treatment."

"What is the military doing with them?"

"The military? More like the company. They're using their DNA and mixing it with humans. It seems their failure with cyborgs wasn't a big enough lesson. They are still determined to mess with human genetics."

"These aliens you're describing don't sound like the original."

"The what?" For some reason Seth's statement formed a ball in her stomach. *Why does that term, original, sound so familiar?* And why couldn't she remember it? She possessed an eidetic memory courtesy of her BCI. Yet, while she possessed a sense of déjà vu, she couldn't put a picture or memory to the word.

Seth frowned. "I thought you retained all your memories."

"I did."

"Yet you don't remember the original? The source? The one they fed us the blood from? The one with the nanos? I'll admit my own recollections are vague. I just remember someone else being in the room, someone who acted as the donor for the nanos. They'd hooked us together, an IV from her to me."

"A woman?"

"I think so. I didn't really get a good look, and like I said, my memories are fuzzy. You don't remember any of that?"

No, but at his words, a haunting plea floated up from her subconscious.

Help me.

The scariest part was she wasn't the one who'd uttered the words. And couldn't have said who did.

Chapter Fifteen

One last time into the past.

A slew of successful missions didn't mean the military was done perfecting their newest breed of soldiers and spies, but they did slacken some of their restrictions. Seth and Anastasia proved a hit as a spy couple, enough so that the military didn't object when they sneaked off to the chapel to get married—her in a borrowed white gown, him in full military uniform. Their honeymoon was spent in the Bahamas, guests of a drug lord. In between hacking the crime boss's computers, disrupting his illegal trade, and killing a few key players, they still managed to have sex in every which way possible, and some that were not humanly possible.

Those were the happiest days of his life. A pity they couldn't last forever.

The doctors, the military, heck everyone except the test subjects themselves, were so giddy with the success of the nanos, they thought it was a great idea to take the modified soldiers to the next level. The problem was the next level involved removing healthy organs and replacing them with mechanical parts. Once Seth found out the plan, he protested, loudly and vigorously.

"What do you mean you're going to replace my heart with a metal one?" He faced off against Dr. Osgoode, unheeding whether his tone bordered on disrespectful. The guy wanted to rip his heart out and replace it with a battery-operated ticker. *He is out of his freaking mind if he thinks I'm going to agree.* This conversation was about to take the same path as the argument he'd had a few weeks before about the doctor's intention to put a computer chip in his head.

"Have you not noticed the dizzy spells and the occasional weakness?"

"Yeah, but I also can't help but notice you're running us like fucking dogs. I mean it's great and all that you want to test our limits, but a body needs to rest a bit sometimes."

"Human bodies do. What we intend to do to yours will make it able to endure more. Sleep will become a thing you do only rarely. Exhaustion will become a thing of the past. When we're done enhancing you, you'll be able to run forever."

"So can a robot. Why do this to humans? More specifically, me?"

"Robots fail. The nanotechnology doesn't work on them. Only bio-organisms can accept the nanos and thrive."

For a moment, an image flashed in Seth's mind, a quick snap of a girl, no, a woman, lying prone on a hospital bed, arms and legs strapped, in the room where they poured liquid fire in his veins. It disappeared just as quickly as it came, and he couldn't pull it up for examination. Seth kept it to himself.

"I've got to say, doc, I'm getting mighty uncomfortable with all this bio-whatchamacallit stuff. It was one thing to stretch the truth and get me to take those nanobots into my body. But now what you're talking about is taking perfectly good organs and replacing them with machine ones, especially my heart. That's getting too extreme even for me. I think it's time we talked about me getting out of the project." The mystery he'd once wanted to unravel had tarnished over the months spent in this veritable dungeon. He was sure he could convince Anastasia to leave with him. He'd not missed the lines of stress as the testing and training got more and more intense—and dangerous.

"Out?" The doctor's tone emerged with a hint of high-pitched incredulity. "What makes you think you can ever leave?"

Seth arched a brow. Was this guy for real? "This isn't Hotel California, dude. I'm an American citizen, which means I'm entitled to a certain thing called my rights. And I have a right to say no to what you plan. Give me a dishonorable discharge if you have to, but I'm done being a guinea pig."

"You'll be done when we say you're done."

Excuse me? Who the hell did this guy think he was telling Seth what he could or could not do with his own life? "No. This ends now." Seth growled the words and loomed over the shorter doctor. It wasn't reassuring to note the little man didn't even flinch. Was he stupid enough to think Seth wouldn't harm him? *Nice guy or not, you can only push me so far before I push back.*

"Stand down, SO101, or you'll regret it."

"My name is Seth, and I'll stand down when you stop being an a-hole. I'm telling you I'm done. I want out of here. Now." He grabbed the shorter man by the lapel of his white coat and hauled him high enough that his feet no longer touched the floor.

A sane man would have cowered. After all, Seth was stronger than a human and trained, courtesy of the doctor and the military, in the art of death. But Dr. Osgoode simply smiled, the satisfied grin of a lizard who opened his disjointed jaw and swallowed his prey whole. "Then I guess we'll do this the hard way. Protocol alpha niner one one. Unit SO101, halt all movement."

Seth froze. Literally. He couldn't move a muscle if he tried, but he could hear and see. *What the fuck is going on?*

"Unit SO101, release me."

Seth's hand opened, and the doctor dropped to the floor with a light thud. As Seth battled the beginnings of panic, Dr. Osgoode smoothed out his lab coat and then smirked. "I'll bet you're wondering what just happened. Remember that brain chip you whined about? The one you said no to a few weeks back? Did I forget to mention we implanted one anyway? We gassed you and your new wife while you slept. You were actually out for several days as your body healed from the incision. Your recuperative abilities are really quite remarkable. You don't even have a scar."

Or a memory of receiving the chip to his brain. This horrified Seth as much as the knowledge his brain now played host to some parasitic technology.

"You never even suspected what we did. You can thank your new enhanced brain for that." The insane little man giggled. "We call the chip a BCI, short for brain computer interface, and while its main purpose is to regulate the nanos, it also does so much more than that. It controls you. You're like a puppet now, just one without strings."

Like hell. No way. What he suggested just wasn't possible. That kind of stuff, it only happened in the movies or books. Not to him.

"I can see you don't believe me. Shall I prove it?" The doctor paused as if to wait for an answer before giggling again, a noise Seth now believed might herald the signs of insanity. "Oops, I forgot, you can't answer. So why don't I show you? Unit SO101, I order you to twerk."

No, not that. Seth would have howled a protest, planted his feet, and categorically refused to perform, but as the doctor had bragged, he no longer controlled his body. Seth was merely a passenger. A horrified and embarrassed onlooker forced to put his bottom up in the air and waggle it while the doctor chortled.

I am so going to kill him for this.

"Unit SO101, assume the at-ease position and freeze." Seth returned to an upright pose, hands looped behind his back, feet slightly apart, and gaze straight ahead. "Fantastic. It works even better than we could have hoped. For now, the BCI's rely on codes and voice recognition. But, soon, when any qualified human gives a command, you'll have to obey. You won't be able to help yourself. You'll be the perfect soldier."

Bastard, you mean I'll be a slave. Seth thought it but couldn't spit it out, much as he wanted to. He just hoped his intense dislike shone through his eyes.

"Right now you're thinking you'll escape the first chance you get. That you can run from me and from this installation."

Actually, he hadn't, but that was probably a good idea.

"And I say, fat chance. By the time we're finished with you, you won't remember a thing. Not the treatments, not this conversation, nothing but what we want you to remember. Which, lucky for you, will be more than some of the others. Given our plans for you require that you be able to act human, you won't have your personality and memories completely wiped like the solider units. We're just going to remove the parts that you don't require, such as what we do here. We can't have our enemies discovering our little secrets."

I am going to kill him slowly and painfully.

"Oh, and you'll be glad to know, you won't be alone. Given your success rate, SO100 will be your partner, which should make you somewhat happy. The pair of you will make the perfect espionage team."

Not Anastasia too. The thought of her becoming a slave to a computer chip did what his own fate couldn't. It gave him strength to fight. Through frozen lips he muttered. "Touch her and die."

The doctor's brows arched. "My, my. That's impressive. How did you manage to speak? I see we still have some tweaking to do to your programming. Or maybe a lesson would be more appropriate. Obey, and we'll leave your new wife unmolested. Disobey and face the consequences."

The doctor's lips curved into an evil smile that didn't bode well at all. "Bring in SO100."

Anastasia walked in of her own free will but faltered at the sight of Seth. Smart girl, she didn't freak out but remained calm. "You wanted to see me, doctor?"

"Hello, Anastasia. I called you here because I need to teach your husband a lesson in co-operation."

"I'm sorry. I don't understand."

"It's really very simple. We intend to replace some of his organs with more efficient mechanical ones."

"You can't do that." She sounded and looked appalled.

"Oh, but we can. And shall. As a matter of fact, if the procedure is successful then we'll also replace most of yours too."

"Like hell," she growled. She lunged, but the doctor had wisely remained out of reach. He uttered his special code before her hands could wring his neck. Anastasia halted, mid motion, but the confusion and panic in her eyes were clear for Seth to see.

"As I explained to your husband, we recently gave you both an upgrade. Nothing major, just a computer chip in the brain to make you more malleable to our needs and to the hardware we need to install. But it seems the BCI might not be enough to keep your other half in line, so we thought we'd provide a live demonstration to remind you of whom you need to obey. Nothing personal. We've just invested too much time and money into this project to let anything like stupid morals and rights get in our way. Are you ready, SO101, for an example of what happens to bad cyborgs who don't obey their masters?"

Seth gritted his teeth and managed to utter, "Fuck you."

"Goodness but you're a strong one. Let's see how long that lasts once you grasp your impotency. Unit SO100, take off your clothes."

What followed was something Seth wished he could forget. He knew Anastasia did because she never referred to that horrifying day. But glimpses of it kept recurring no matter what they did to him, no matter how many times they scanned and wiped him to remove all traces of the lab and experiments. That moment returned in flashes to him or in dreams, and eventually, he remembered it in excruciating detail; every pained and fearful gaze in her eyes, every degrading thing they did to her to ensure his obedience. Was it any wonder the first thing he did when he went rogue was to hunt those soldiers down and kill them? Painfully.

Unfortunately for him, the doctor slipped his grasp. But Seth never stopped looking. *And when I find him, he'll wish he'd never been born.*

In spite of the memory wipes, everything changed that day, and not just because they replaced his heart with an eternal metal ticker and his liver with a more efficient filtration processor. Something in them, in their psyche or their emotions, got tainted or twisted. After those modifications and the day they tried to wipe from his mind, things changed, not just within him but between him and Anastasia.

As the doctor promised, Anastasia forgot what happened. They both did. For a time.

Eventually Seth remembered, but by then, he and Anastasia had gone their separate ways.

Things never quite worked out after the moment that changed him from a slightly enhanced human to full-on cyborg. He couldn't have pinpointed why though. Even once he got his memories back, while he could see where it all started to go wrong, he couldn't figure out the why, although he suspected the military played a part.

Sure they still had sex and laughed and talked, but something seemed different. She seemed different. She had holes in her memory, holes he learned not to prod because she became very agitated, and, in one case, she scared the shit out of him because she shut down.

She wasn't the only one with gaps. At the time, he didn't notice them, probably because the military or asshats in charge made him forget, but once he got control of his mind back, he spent time analyzing and filtering that lost time. He came to the conclusion that outside forces were at work, plotting against him and Anastasia, but to what purpose? Wouldn't it have been simpler to just order them apart?

By the time he woke in a strange bed, his memories of how he got there blank, Natasha the spy looming over him with a triumphant leer, things had gotten tense.

Anastasia had withdrawn into herself and become almost mechanical in her actions and gestures, secretive in her thoughts. Her jealousy had also spiraled out of control on several occasions, which was why when Natasha said she'd gotten what she wanted, a sensation of dread filled him.

It didn't entirely surprise him when Anastasia confronted him, gun in hand, tears streaming down her face, intent on killing him.

And despite her not pulling the trigger, a part of him did die. It died because no matter how much he loved her, and she loved him—*I know she did*—the military had ruined it. Ruined them both. No longer were they in control of their lives, their destinies. Heck, Seth barely controlled his body or his mind.

As for Anastasia? It was a wonder she didn't immediately pull the trigger. He could tell her machine side warred with her human, urging her to obey and kill.

Not wanting her to live with the guilt, he did the easy thing, and yet the hardest. He left.

But it didn't mean he stopped loving. He couldn't help but dream and remember the girl with the bright eyes and spitfire attitude who'd climbed the wall. The woman he'd set off on an adventure with. The woman who'd stolen his heart, owned his soul, and without whom life lost meaning and color.

A woman the galaxy had in its inexplicable actions brought back to him. For a second chance.

Chapter Sixteen

Back to the future, this time to stay.

Despite Seth's constant flirting and teasing within the privacy of their minds, they didn't manage to find time alone. On the contrary, between keeping Jerry happy, her commanding officer from grumbling, and maintaining her cover, Anastasia barely saw Seth, but that didn't mean she wasn't aware of him.

Despite his initial balking at his task, she heard through the grapevine about the handsome explorer she'd rescued who was flirting like crazy with the head of the chemical science division. It seemed Seth was playing hard to get, but not so hard that Stanley, his target, was giving up. On the contrary, the wagering among the crew was how long John/Seth could keep him at arm's length before capitulating. He'd already managed to get nicer quarters and brand new clothing instead of recycled uniforms like the rest of the grunts. He was dining with the officers on board instead of in the cafeteria, and, in general, having a lot more fun than her. Was it any wonder when she finally ran into Seth in the flesh that her tone was less than genial?

"Why if it isn't the lady who saved me," Seth exclaimed when he came across her in the hall.

Her lips pursed, mostly in annoyance at herself because, despite her constant inner conviction that she wanted nothing to do with the man, every time she saw him, her defective metal heart skipped a damned beat—and her libido kicked into overdrive.

So unfair. She'd fought hard to forget him over the years, to build a life for herself. Perhaps she didn't exactly bask in happiness, not like she'd once enjoyed and briefly touched again during their reunion, but she wasn't about to throw all she'd accomplished away on something she couldn't have.

And what exactly is stopping me? She couldn't blame Jerry for her reticence. She knew she didn't love him, so he wasn't the one holding her back. It wasn't a lack of attraction. One wink, one word, one touch from Seth, and she turned to putty. So why did she not cave at his thinly veiled attempts to win her back? What was she scared of?

I fear nothing. Except the heartache she'd never quite recovered from. Sure, their relationship had cooled during the many missions they'd gone on. The military, she could see now, had done its best to plant the seeds of doubt even before the final fiasco. When she'd thought Seth betrayed her, she'd gone through an agony worse than even her transformation into a cyborg. To find out that she had been manipulated into believing it? It not only added fuel to the burning need for vengeance but also reinforced her belief that they could never recapture what they'd once enjoyed. *How could he ever forgive me for doubting him? How can I ever forgive myself?* Perhaps she'd not loved him enough to recognize the truth.

All of this passed through her mind in less than a second, not long enough for anyone to notice, but him. He could always read her. At the silent query in her mind, *Is everything all right?*, she didn't reply, not via wireless at any rate. She stuck to keeping things public and impersonal. "John, how nice to see you. I trust you are settling in comfortably?"

"Marvelously so. I have to say the crew on board has been most accommodating. Especially a certain gent by the name of Stanley. Why, we're planning a lovely evening, just the two of us with some imported earth foods, wine and *talk*." He winked.

Letting her BCI handle a mundane conversation aloud, she switched to internal speech to ask the real questions. *This hall is clean of microphones, but just in case, let's keep this short. Have you gotten anything yet?*

Not quite. But tonight is the night.

So you implied. How far are you going to go? And will you be on top or the bottom? She couldn't help but internally smirk.

Kinky girl. Wouldn't you like to know?

Actually I would. I've got a decent chunk of credits riding on this. The pot on that and the exact time has gotten huge.

You're wagering on me getting lucky with Stanley? Despite their mundane outward conversation, he arched a brow at her inner jibe.

Just trying to blend in with the humans.

You're a sick woman. I love it!

Freak.

I'll take that as a compliment. Back to the evening I've got planned. After a little dinner and a little conversation,

I plan to adjourn with my special friend whereupon he shall fall into a trance-like state.

And why will he be in a trance-like state?

Because of the drug I plan to slip him of course. I smuggled a vial of hypnotic serum from your boyfriend's lab. He's got some disturbing shit going on in there.

Disturbing how? Was he experimenting on a cyborg? Despite her claims to Seth that she wouldn't blow her cover, it had bothered her when she found out about the testing. She'd done her best over the years to slyly intervene, such as falsifying results or changing a cyborg status from active to defective, which meant the cyber unit in question got shipped to a remote outpost to be used as slave labor. Not an ideal situation, but better than the alternative.

No, he wasn't getting freaky with one of our kind, but I took the time to read the labels on some of his stuff and peek through his files. All I gotta say is, once we blow this joint, it might be a good idea to make sure he and that lab are dismantled first. It's in need of a serious nuking. He's delving into some pretty heavy territory, most of it real bad for us.

Are you sure? He keeps talking about how his tests are failures and whining about his inability to break through.

Then he's either lacking some serious self-esteem when it comes to his work, he's an idiot, or he's fucking with you. What's wrong? Haven't been putting out lately?

For your information, our relationship isn't about sex.

I know. He's been bitching about it. How smug Seth sounded, even in wireless mode.

He's what?

Apparently he's getting tired of your sealed thighs, which is why he's been banging a private who works in the engine room.

Why that two-timing asshat!

Jealous?

No. But, still, is it that hard for a man to keep it in his pants and show a little restraint? We are, after all, dating.

I'd point out the irony and flaws in your statement, but we don't have time. I need to get ready for my date.

Are you sure this hypno drug is going to work? And what about after? How much will he remember? Should I plan for an immediate evac?

Nope. If all goes well, loverboy will wake in the morning believing he had the time of his life. I shall break up with him so as to avoid any further contact and possibility of triggering a memory. And, at the first way station, we come to, we shall disembark to continue on our quest.

Only if needed. Once we know the location of the company headquarters, we can re-evaluate.

Oh we shall because if I have to go one more day without touching you I might just explode.

Excuse me.

You heard me, wife. I miss you.

I'm right here.

No you're not. Our bodies might be having a mundane conversation, I might be able to see you, but I'm not with you. And I need you. Need to touch you. Kiss you.

His words aroused a longing in her for the same thing, a longing she kept trying to deny but couldn't quite stifle. But she tried. *I've told you I'm not interested in becoming a couple again, or being with you.*

Liar. You can't tell me you're not missing me too.

How did he know? She kept trying to ignore it, but the unmistakable fact was she missed him. Irritating as he was, distracting, fun, intelligent, and so much more. She missed their intimate moments, and not just those without clothing.

Unlike the other humans on board, she could be herself with him. She didn't have to lie or adopt a persona or pretend. To him, she was Anastasia. Cybernetic organism, part machine, part woman. He knew her past, was determined to be part of her present, and wanted to plan for a future. He was everything she wanted in a man. Everything she'd missed, and without the lie she'd used to push him away so long ago, a possibility that frightened her.

Now is not the time to discuss this.

Then plan a time because I'm getting tired of waiting and faking it. It's time we reclaimed our lives, time I reclaimed you ... wife.

And, with that bold statement, he saluted her and walked away, and this time, she was the one watching his sweet ass.

Chapter Seventeen

Ever get the feeling that something wasn't right? Seth had that feeling as he sat at a table set for two in Stanley's private chambers. But why? A true cyborg would dismiss the sensation or file it under illogical. Some cyborgs would even check themselves in for a full diagnostic, assuming something was defective with their programming. Seth, though, knew better than to ignore the human instincts remaining to him. Some things even science and math, and even the best BCI, couldn't explain. Although he tried.

He first attempted to analyze the situation and pinpoint what was setting off internal warning bells. Romantic setting with holographic candlelight, a red blanket turned into a tablecloth, and subtle, soothing music in the background. His date had made an effort to look nice with freshly ironed slacks, a button shirt, and freshly washed hair that showed signs still of moisture. On the surface, things appeared perfect, and yet ...

Despite Stanley's aggressive pursuit of him, now that they were alone, the man appeared nervous, easily evidenced by his sweaty palms, rapid chattering nonsense, and the way he kept bobbing up from his seat to fetch things. Seth almost had to wonder if he'd misread the signs. Perhaps Stanley wasn't as ripe for picking as he'd thought. Perhaps the guy was all about the public show. Or he was just genuinely nervous about their first time together. A pity Seth couldn't put his mind at ease and let him know nothing would happen. This dinner and supposed seduction was just a ruse to get the guy alone. On the one hand, Stanley's distraction made it easy to slip something into his drink; on the other, the frustrating man never sipped enough to get him into the trance state Seth required.

"Is something the matter?" he finally asked, twirling his own wine glass, an extravagance in space. Most of the items allowed on board tended toward the sturdy side, given replacing them was so difficult and expensive.

"Wrong?" Stanley's reply emerged high-pitched and guilty sounding. Seth's danger meter rocketed up several notches. "Nope. Nothing is wrong."

He's lying. Was it simply nerves about the planned evening? Could it be that, despite Stanley's interest in Seth as a partner, he wasn't very experienced when it came to the actual intimate part of the relationship? Possible. But, still, this level of unease seemed extreme, especially given Stanley was the one who'd planned this intimate evening.

"Why don't you sit down? Have a drink with me? Relax. We have all evening to *talk*," Seth purred, adding a little wine to his own glass before shaking it at his date.

He took a sip then another as Stanley finally perched himself, a nervous animal ready to take flight at the first sign of motion.

Would you drink the wine already! If Seth wasn't worried his target would remember, he'd have forced it down his gullet. As it was, he had to smile and play the part of interested lover, drinking away at the bitter vintage, which was more vinegar than wine.

Oddly enough, the crappy alcohol had more of an effect than expected. Which is to say, Seth actually felt it.

What the hell?

Usually his nanos took care of any inebriation unless he specifically ordered them to stand down. Not this time. Despite his BCI requesting immediate nullification of the wine, his body felt heavy, sluggish. He opened his mouth to speak, and his tongue wouldn't cooperate. He could only blink as his body refused to obey and gravity tugged him. He landed face first on the floor, paralyzed.

But aware.

He drugged me! Someway, somehow, the fucking jerk he'd strung along had found a way to incapacitate him, which meant—

"Stupid cyborg."

—he knew his secret. *This is really not good.* Seth's second thought was he needed to warn Anastasia. However, much like his body refused to cooperate, so did his BCI. No matter how he strained to send a message, it failed. Wireless transmission was out.

"You almost had me fooled," said a not-so-nervous Stanley. On the contrary, now that he'd rendered Seth into a cognizant statue, he assumed a cocky tone and attitude.

You just wait until the effects wear off, you little prick. I'm going to wipe that smug smile off your face and find out the location of the company while I'm at it.

Multitasking, something all cyborgs excelled at.

"I have to admit to being most excited you fell into our laps. Or my lap, I should say. You're the first spy model we've managed to recover, and while I'd read the reports, I have to admit I'd not realized just how human you would seem. Or how advanced compared to the other models I've been working with. Passing metal detectors and the cyborg body scanners we've had built into our medical equipment? I have to say, that's very clever. We'll have to examine you very closely to see how you did it so we can prevent cyborgs from infiltrating in the future. We can't have you learning our secrets."

If the scanners didn't give me away, what the fuck did?

Lucky for him, he got an answer. "You might have managed to pull off whatever diabolical plot you had in mind if not for one thing. Someone recognized you. And quite by chance. We took on some passengers last night, more like evacuees. It seems our plans to rendezvous with one of our experimentation facilities came too late. Some of your friends got there first and destroyed it."

Booyah! Seth did a mental fist pump.

"But it wasn't the most vital one, and at least its lead scientists and administrators made it out alive. My brother, Arthur, was one of them. You probably don't know him. But, from what I understand, you know our grandfather. Dr. Osgoode."

Funny how no matter how much of him they'd transformed, that name could still make Seth's blood run cold.

"I happened to tell Arthur about you and showed him an image. He thought you seemed familiar and sent that picture to granddad. Imagine my shock when I found out that you aren't John Tweed at all, but unit SO101. A cyborg spy model."

A spy who'd been outed by the one enemy he'd never managed to find. Fuck.

"I'll admit you both surprised and excited me. And when I say excite, I'm not talking about your good looks. On the contrary, you could look like a troll, and I'd still be in heaven. The things I could do to you to advance my research. The knowledge your body and brain hides." Stanley sighed. "Alas, it seems granddad has missed having you around. Lucky for you, or not I guess depending on your view, you've been commandeered. A squad of soldiers is on its way to place you in stasis so we can safely transport you to granddad's laboratory."

Safely? Ha. That was what the little prick thought. *I beg to differ.* Seth's baby finger twitched. Not much but enough to let him know his nanos, while sluggish at the moment, were working at freeing him from whatever drug Stanley had concocted. It seemed granddad and dear old Stanley weren't aware that the freed cyborgs, unlike their captured brethren, had spent the last few years improving their programming. Adapting and advancing, always striving for improvement to keep themselves from being made slaves again. These modifications would play to his advantage, if given enough time.

What a pity he wasn't going to have much of it.

The buzzer for the room rang out, and Stanley uttered an oral command for the door to open.

I need to get my nanos to wake up and take care of the sedative before it's too late. Seth flexed a finger. Two fingers. He heard more than saw the bodies taking up position around him. He didn't pay much attention, not when all of his focus needed to be on regaining control of his body. Unbeknownst to them, his muscles tingled as they shook off the temporary stupor. He didn't let it show though, not even when he heard a gasp of feminine surprise when they rolled him to his back and a bevy of guns was aimed at his head.

It seemed Stanley had invited an audience. Awesome. He'd give them something to remember, even if it would prove short-lived. Muscle functions came back on line with a slowness that grated. He wasn't quite ready to make his move. But he was close. So close. So—

He heard Anastasia's voice and had to scrap his half-assed plan to take out the ring of guards around him. *What is she doing here?*

Whatever her motivation for showing up, his mission oriented wife, who swore she wanted nothing to do with him, did the one thing he never expected. She came to his rescue.

Chapter Eighteen

Things on board the ship turned chaotic overnight. Refugees from the planet they were supposed to rendezvous with came aboard with wild tales of marauding cyborgs—score for the home team!—and brought along specimens that required guarding, along with a whole lot of disorder that Anastasia could have done without. But none of that compared to the more worrisome news that Seth's cover was compromised.

Jerry spilled the beans. "You won't believe this," he exclaimed. "But we've caught one of the infamous spy models."

"Say again?" Anastasia looked up from her tray of cafeteria grub—off-white bland mashed potatoes covered in a lumpy brown sauce served with a hunk of something she preferred not to analyze with desiccated looking green peas.

"I said we caught a spy model, or are about to. Stanley's drugging him as we speak."

"Cyborgs can't be drugged." She spoke without thinking, but Jerry didn't catch her adamant claim, probably because it was common knowledge that human drugs didn't work on cyber units. Or didn't used to.

The smug look on Jerry's face indicated otherwise. "They can now. I developed the formula to paralyze the bastards while you were gone."

"And didn't tell me?" She couldn't hide the accusatory tone.

"I was still running tests to make sure. But I've finally found a way to temporarily stop the nanos from doing their nullifying act to drugging agents, which in turn means we can incapacitate cyborgs long enough for us to terminate them."

"Holy shit." Where Jerry took her expletive as praise, she, on the other hand, meant it more as holy-shit-we're-in-bigger-fucking-trouble-than-we-thought. She also kicked herself now too for not having taken care of Jerry before this. Seth had mentioned the man was more dangerous than she thought, that he knew more than he admitted, and she'd foolishly not caught on. Because of her failure to properly judge a target, now Seth would pay the price.

"So they're going to kill him?"

"He's too dangerous to leave loose." Jerry's eyes glittered with malice. "Cyborgs are an abomination that need to be stopped by any means necessary. Don't you think?"

I think I should have torn your head off and used it as a soccer ball a long time ago, but regret wouldn't save her stupid husband. Meanwhile, Jerry waited for a reply. "Cyborgs are monsters."

His smile widened. "I'm so glad you agree. Would you believe there are some that think they're just misunderstood and deserving of a second chance? They're so misguided they even formed a group under the leadership of one of those inhuman bots."

"Really? I'd not heard about that." Not entirely true. She'd heard rumors, but thought nothing of them. A cyborg on earth was one obviously bent on suicide. Any group formed with a cyber-unit at its head would be short lived at best.

"The media has been keeping it hush hush so as to not panic the population. But this group exists alright and is being run by some cyborg calling himself Adam."

Adam? Interesting because she'd once known an Adam. No way. It had to be a coincidence. It couldn't be the same one. But, then again, the cyborg world was a small one and she'd not spent much time on earth lately, nor had she spoken to Adam in quite some time. Something she should perhaps rectify.

Once she completed her current mission, she'd have to look into this group. If Adam was indeed in charge and had managed to wrangle some human supporters, then maybe there was a chance for cyborgs to eventually live in the open. Or at least tell the world the truth so that their sad story wouldn't get repeated. "Does he have many followers?"

"Enough that he's going to need taking care of. The problem has been infiltrating his group. They've proven wily so far. Or so I hear. It's why my work is so important. The higher-ups want to capture him and make a public example of him, but to do so, we need to make sure we can control him first."

Damn, this was all bad news and information Seth and the others needed to be made aware of. Just one big problem. Seth was about to get his ass taken out.

Jerry's wristband pinged, and he cast a brief glance to the display. "And the cyborg is down. The drug worked. If you'll excuse me, I volunteered to join the extermination squad. I want to see the effects of my work first-hand."

"You're going there right now? Can I come?" The request slipped out of her.

"Of course you can." As if they were going on a lovely picnic instead of an execution, Jerry tucked her hand in his arm and led her toward Stanley's quarters. They joined a group of armed soldiers on the way.

Smoke practically poured from her ears as Anastasia analyzed the situation furiously. What to do? What to do! If she moved to protect Seth, she'd blow her cover. *But I can't let them kill him.*

At the same time, making a move to defend him meant they'd be fighting to get off the ship, a ship in the middle of space, filled to the brim with humans, many of them armed. No matter which way she calculated it, the odds came out against them.

Cyborgs were impressive fighters. They could take on huge numbers of enemies at a time and emerge victorious, but even she and Seth—if Seth recovered in time from the drug—couldn't hope to prevail against an entire military craft of armed soldiers and scientists like Jerry, with cyborg elimination experiments at hand.

What else, other than this so-called drug, does he have at his disposal?

She still hadn't made up her mind when they entered the room at the heels of the military squad. The scene that greeted her made her gasp.

On the floor, splayed in an ignoble heap, face buried in the synthetic fiber flooring, was Seth. Stanley leered in triumph as he rolled his drugged date onto his back.

She couldn't help but gasp when Seth's face came into view. His vivid blue eyes were open and staring, but when she tried to send a wireless message, it bounced back. It seemed his BCI wasn't receiving. But she'd wager he was well aware of his surroundings and events, and probably cursing them.

The military grunts advanced on him, laser pistols out and aimed. Seth didn't budge. Jerry snickered at her back. Stanley grinned and rubbed his hands in glee. Talk about an unfolding nightmare.

A trio of soldiers held their guns aimed at Seth while a fourth positioned himself at his head, gun aimed for a fatal shot. She had only a split second to decide her next move.

They can't kill him. Things couldn't end this way. Not after everything they'd gone through together. They'd just found each other again. She'd only just realized how the military had played a part in splitting them up. She needed him. Loved him. But the situation was impossible. She couldn't save them both. If she acted, they'd both die.

But rationality couldn't control her. Even if she was more machine than flesh, her human emotions still ruled a major part of her, and that part refused to let the man she loved die. Without warning, not even a battle cry, Anastasia lunged.

The first soldier slumped to the floor without a sound, which probably had to do with the fact she snapped his neck so quickly he never had time to voice a protest.

The second soldier managed a startled, "What the fuck?" before the kick she aimed at his gun-toting hand shattered his wrist. He dropped his weapon with a strident scream. *Bet you he wishes he could turn off his pain receptors like a cyborg now,* she thought with cold malice.

The third gun-toting military grunt became the recipient of her famed left hook, but she didn't pause to admire the blood as it spattered over a shocked Stanley, who watched the unfolding events with his mouth gaping. She had to keep moving before they had time to react.

The fourth soldier hesitated a moment too long, trying to decide between targets—her or Seth. Idiot. Logic said active dangers were of higher priority than comatose ones. But, then again, how could she expect a simple human to understand that? He died still trying to make up his mind.

Which made the jab at the base of her spine the more inexplicable.

I incapacitated all the enemies. So who stabbed her? And why was she falling to the floor, oops, not anymore. A hand caught her by the hair and kept her from sinking all the way.

"I can't believe I was dating a fucking cyborg bitch. That explains why I couldn't pry her damned thighs apart." Jerry's nasty remark barely made its way through the fog in her head.

The jerk drugged me!

It seemed she'd made more than one miscalculation about her boyfriend. She could almost hear Seth's mocking, *Told you so.*

And, wow, was the drug ever freaking potent. Her eyes blinked, once, twice, threeeeeeee …

Chapter Nineteen

Awareness returned instantly, but it didn't come without questions. *Where am I?* The last thing Anastasia recalled, she'd taken care of the soldiers threatening Seth then—

That fucking prick Jerry had drugged her!

Some boyfriend he turned out to be. It seemed she'd not fooled him as thoroughly as she'd thought. Something must have warned him that she was more than just human. It seemed obvious now that she analyzed the situation. He'd intentionally baited her with Seth's demise, waiting to see if she'd react and confirm his suspicions.

How she wanted to have her programming checked for having fallen into his neatly laid trap. She also wanted revenge. Once she got her hands on him, she'd kill him, slowly, and painfully. But, first, she needed out of the cryogenic capsule she found herself encased in.

While she'd never been an occupant of one before, she'd observed enough of them from the outside to recognize where she currently found herself. Coffin shape, tight squeeze, tubes inserted in her body, filtering nutrients and drugs into her body. Good thing she didn't suffer from claustrophobia, or she might have panicked. However, not fearing small spaces didn't mean she didn't feel trepidation. The heavy shielding on the casing prevented her from wirelessly accessing any networks.

The biggest question running through her mind, though, was in whose custody did she reside? Was she still on board the military ship with Jerry and Stanley, the walking dead men? Was she about to become the newest test subject at a company laboratory? Or did someone else have her in their possession, because the face peering at her through the fogged glass was not one she recognized and, with his unshaven jaw and shaggy hair, didn't appear to belong to either the military or the geek crew the company usually hired.

With a hiss and a few mechanical clicks, the lid to the capsule popped open.

Limbs still sluggish meant she couldn't grab him by the throat and choke him for answers so she had to settle for a fierce scowl and snarled, "Who the hell are you?"

"MJ. And you are?"

Ha, like she'd tell him anything until she got a better grasp on the situation. "What the fuck happened?" was the next question out of her mouth, followed by, "Where's Seth?"

The stranger, not at all perturbed by her profanity or attitude, fiddled over the capsule's tubes and control panel. He spared her a brief glance. "What happened? I was kind of hoping you'd tell us. Why were you frozen? Who are you? And how do you know Seth? Is he in one of the capsules as well?"

"How I know him and who I am are none of your business." But she found it interesting that this MJ knew of Seth. It was the only reason she didn't immediately kill him. He might have answers she needed, such as where her husband was.

She yanked at the tubes still sticking out of her skin, determined to find out for herself what the hell was going on.

"Hey, what are you doing? We have to do this carefully lest you accidentally bleed out …" The man in the stained medical coat tapered off, his eyes tracking the way her wounds sealed shut, cutting off the sluggish flow of blood. "You're a cyborg."

"In the flesh, or not. Depends on your perspective." She bared her teeth in a feral smile.

He didn't flinch or run. Brave fellow. "You're a female cyborg."

"Duh. Was it my tits that gave it away?" was her sarcastic retort.

"Are all the capsule occupants cyborg?"

"I have no idea. Like I said, I don't even know how I got in one to start with."

"I don't know the how, but I can tell you that we found you on a military vessel in cahoots with the company. They ambushed us in space, but we managed to turn the tables on them. Unfortunately, the ship self destructed before we could discover too much. But not before we managed to salvage a few things, like these here capsules. There were originally six in total, but we only managed to recover five before the ship exploded into space debris."

Not all the capsules survived? An icy feeling gripped her. It couldn't be fear. She'd conquered that emotion a long time ago. Tell that to her frantically racing heart, clammy hands, and the fluttery panic in her stomach. She pushed past the stranger, unheeding her nudity as she scanned the room.

Not much to see. She appeared to be in some kind of medical area, an outdated one given most of the equipment bore a layer of dust and an air of disuse.

Spotting the other capsules, she strode to the first one and peered through the glass. The haze over the window wouldn't give her a clear view. She began typing on its keypad, looking for information on its occupant. Data streamed by on the small electronic screen. None of it jumped out at her, so she moved onto the next. And the next. On the third, she spotted something in the flow of information that had her releasing a pent-up breath. "I think this is him."

She didn't even realize she'd spoken aloud until MJ pushed her aside and said, "Let me take care of this. It's kind of tricky. The military or company, whoever encased you in these cryo chambers, didn't want you woken up. They put some intricate traps in place meant to kill the sleeper if you're not careful in the thawing process."

With her hands shaking, her mind a muddle, and fear still an unpleasant companion, she stepped aside and let the doctor do his thing. Killing Seth because of her irrational need to see him safe would not do either of them any good, although she'd like to know when he suddenly became so important again in the grand scheme of her life.

What happened to just using him and ditching him when I was done? Or the better question, now that she believed him when he said he never strayed, now that she was almost one hundred percent certain her mind had been messed with, why was she so afraid to give him back her heart? *It is I who betrayed him in the end.* But would admitting her mistake and asking for forgiveness accomplish anything?

Logic said Seth deserved better than her and the blatant disregard she'd shown. Not to mention, she still had a quest to finish. A quest perhaps forever out of reach with her carefully cultivated cover ruined.

The lid to the capsule popped open a crack. Gases escaped with an ominous hiss. Anastasia crowded close and breathed an audible sigh of relief as Seth's slumbering face appeared amidst the fog.

"Is he going to be okay?" she asked as the stranger kept punching at the keypad.

"It's Seth. Short of a nuke or decapitation, I doubt anything could kill him."

"You know him?"

"Just about every cyborg does. He's played a huge part in our liberation. And driven just about everyone nuts at one point or another."

"That sounds like Seth." And confirmed her guess that the man who'd released her was a cyborg, which meant he got to live.

"From your tone, I'm going to guess you're acquainted, and not just recently."

"We've known each other a long time. We were changed around the same time period."

"And you are?"

"Anastasia."

"My wife." While said in a drowsy, gravelly tone, there was no mistaking Seth's words.

The relief was instant. She didn't think. She acted—and slugged him in the gut.

"Ow," Seth grunted. One eyelid peeled open, and a blue orb squinted at her. "What was that for?"

"For being such a jerk." *And for scaring me into admitting I still love and need you.*

"And here I would have called myself chivalrous for volunteering to enter one of these sleep coffins so you wouldn't wake up alone."

She froze. "You did what?"

"Well, what did you expect me to do? I mean you did, after all, come to my rescue like some wondrous galaxy Valkyrie. Your moves were like something out of The Matrix. Smooth and deadly. I really thought you were going to single handedly rescue us, and then your prick of a boyfriend jabbed you with a needle. I guess he used the same drug on you that they used on me."

"You saw all that and yet did nothing?" she interrupted. "I could have used a hand."

"Hey, I was still recovering, and I didn't want to get in your way."

She glared at him.

"Okay, so I enjoyed the show. Sue me. Do you know how long it's been since I got to admire someone with your skill level when it comes to a fight?"

She couldn't help but preen at his praise. "Fight? Ha. I took those guys out before they could even fire a shot."

"Exactly. It was poetry in motion." Seth sighed.

MJ snorted. "I see being frozen hasn't fixed his warped sense of humor."

"Now I really believe you when you say you know him," she muttered.

"MJ and I go way back," Seth said with a grin. "He loves me."

"I'd love you better if you were mute," grumbled MJ.

"We all would. But not until I get the rest of his story." She poked Seth. "Go on. You still haven't gotten to the part where you ended up a Popsicle. Let me guess, Jerry drugged you with a second syringe?"

"Not exactly. He stabbed you and grabbed you by the hair, which, I'll admit, made me a little mad, but I didn't get truly pissed until he squeezed your boob. I was understandably a tad upset. No man enjoys having his woman groped, just like no husband should ever tolerate anyone ogling their bare-assed wife. Which reminds me, MJ, please give my wife something to cover herself, lest I have to remove your eyes for having gazed upon her naked splendor." Seth might have made the request in a light tone, but the coldness in his eyes said, "Do it or else!"

"Your wife?" MJ couldn't hide his incredulity.

"Yes, my wife. Didn't I already mention that? A wife that, I might add, you've seen naked, which I find myself not liking one bit. So I suggest if you want to keep your head intact you offer her an item of clothing."

Unable to hide his astonishment, while at the same time biting back a grin, MJ stripped off his white coat and handed it to her.

"Thank you, MJ. I would have disliked having to kill you."

"Ha, says the man who can barely twitch his baby finger right now."

While Anastasia slipped on the coat, Seth and MJ bantered back and forth, the teasing conversation of friends, with violent tendencies. While amusing—especially when MJ threatened to purple nurple Seth while he was still half frozen—she had questions. "If you guys are done playing my penis is bigger than yours, could we get back to how the hell we ended up as coffin Popsicles."

"As mentioned, I got a bit upset when your boyfriend grabbed your tit."

MJ interrupted. "Hold on, I thought you said she was your wife. You let your wife date other men?"

"I was undercover," she said. "And we are separated."

"We had a misunderstanding," Seth added.

"It's complicated."

"I'll say," MJ replied, followed by a low whistle. "I've got a super brain, and I'm having problems following."

"Suffice it to say, we had a bit of a squabble and went our separate ways for a few years. Now we're reunited and determined to make things work."

"He is. I still want a divorce." At Seth's stern glare, she smirked. Love him or not, she wasn't about to give in too easily. A man like Seth enjoyed a challenge. It was what kept their relationship fresh.

"We'll discuss this later," Seth promised.

"Whatever. Right now, I'm still waiting to hear what the fuck happened. How come you managed to shake off the drug? Jerry seemed pretty sure it would knock you out and for a while."

"Ha. As if. I am cyborg. Nothing can take me down permanently."

"Except for a well-aimed laser cut or sword," MJ interjected.

"Why must you all persist in such pessimism?" Seth moaned with a roll of his eyes.

"It's called recognizing our limits, idiot. Now back to the drugs. How come it affected me so much worse than you? We both received the same upgrades. We both have the same nanos."

"Ah, but mine have since been modified by Einstein. The military and company aren't the only ones with scientists. We've been working on improving our resistance and immunity."

"You just always have to one-up me," she grumbled. "So, if you're so impervious, how did you end up being captured? I would have thought you'd have fought your way clear and escaped into space. Why the hell did you give yourself up?"

"Simple, dear wife. They would have killed you. As soon as Jerry threatened your life, I agreed to their terms."

By all the titanium in her body, he'd managed to shock her. He'd let them turn him into an ice cube to save her? Oh how she loved him. "You jerk. Why must you keep doing things like that?"

"Like what?"

"Things that show you care and value me. How am I supposed to hate you?" She slugged him in the gut again before whirling to stomp off. She changed her mind before she took a single step and did a complete three-sixty. Leaning forward, she plastered her mouth to his after a whispered, "Thank you."

But she didn't let him enjoy the embrace for long before she tore her lips away. "Don't think this means anything."

A twinkle in his eyes went well with the curve of his lips as he replied, "I would never think to presume with you."

"Good."

"Um, if you're both done, may I finish unhooking Seth here and check his vitals?"

While MJ completed the unfreezing process, ripping the tubes out and letting Seth's body seal over the holes, her husband fired some questions at him. "What ship are we on?"

"The *SSBiteMe*."

"Seriously?" she interjected. "All the cool names in the universe you could choose from and you choose that? Your idea, I presume."

Seth laughed. "Not this time. That distinction belongs to Aramus, the ship's commander. I assume he's on board?"

MJ nodded. "Yes, but—"

"I'm surprised he's not here supervising."

"Well, you see—"

"Is he on the command deck?"

"No, his quarters, but you really shouldn't—"

"Say hello to my bestest friend in the whole universe?"

"Your best friend has a girlfriend and doesn't want to be disturbed."

The slap to MJ's head didn't even rock him, but he wasn't happy about it nonetheless. "What the fuck was that for?"

"You obviously have a screw loose. I was trying to fix you," Seth replied in a matter-of-fact tone.

"No loose screws. Aramus really has a girlfriend."

"Like fuck! This I have to see." Pulling free of the rest of the wires, Seth stepped out of the cryogenic coffin and went straight to a cabinet, where he pulled forth a pair of pants. He also tossed her a smaller pair. "Cover up your girl parts," he commanded. "This isn't a nudist ship."

"Says the guy going topless."

"You'll need to control yourself, as there's no time to cover my impressive upper body. I have to go document this rare and probably short-lived event. Aramus with a girlfriend." Seth snorted. With that comment, Seth strode off, leaving a dumbstruck MJ to gape after him.

"Oh, this won't be good," mumbled the cyborg doctor.

Anastasia cocked her head. "What do you mean? I thought they were friends."

"Kind of, if you consider Aramus' threats to kill him 'friendly'."

"I think death threats and Seth go hand in hand."

"True. But this time, Seth could end up going too far. Aramus hasn't been the same since he met this girl."

"Are you saying there's something defective with this Aramus fellow?"

"Not really, unless you count the fact the biggest, orneriest bastard of a cyborg alive finally admitted he was capable of caring."

"Why is that so surprising?"

"Because the woman he fell for is human, and Aramus hates them. And, by hate, I mean he'd nuke them all in a blink of an eye and not feel an ounce of remorse."

"Is this your way of saying this woman is in danger?" Anastasia might not agree with what some humans did, but she wouldn't stand by and watch one be abused.

"No, she's not in danger, but Seth might be if he interrupts Aramus at the wrong moment. He's very protective of Riley and, given his mixed feelings on Seth, could react violently." MJ shrugged. "When it comes to jealousy, we have no control it seems."

Something she knew all too well. "My husband, ever the idiot. Which way to this Aramus' quarters? I'd better head him off."

Because she hadn't saved him then had him save her and then gotten defrosted only to lose him to a jealous cyborg. *This saving his stupid ass gig is starting to become a habit.* Just like the old days. By all the nanos in her body, it was good to have him back.

Chapter Twenty

Whistling a jaunty tune, Seth waved and said hello to the cyborgs he saw on his way to Aramus' quarters. Most stared at him dumbstruck. It might have been his lack of shoes and shirt. Maybe it was his grin and the fact that he ran, staying out of reach of Anastasia, who shot irritated mind commands at him; *Halt your stupid, mischief-making ass right this instant.*

As if. He rather enjoyed having her chase him. Besides, he really wanted to see Aramus. The grumpy bastard was, whether he liked it or not, one of Seth's best friends, and he'd probably been worried sick at Seth's disappearance. *I'm just being a good ol' buddy and reassuring him of my wellbeing.* Nah. He just wanted to meet the woman nuts enough to get cozy with Aramus.

The lock code on Aramus' room took but a few seconds for him to break through. The door swished open, and Seth strode in, only to stop dead. For a moment he wondered if his eyes were defective or whether they'd entered a wormhole during his sleep and crossed over to an alternate universe. Something cataclysmic must have happened because there was Aramus, in bed, with a human! MJ spoke the truth.

Holy shit. Somewhere in the universe, pigs flew.

"Seth!" Aramus snapped out his name. "Where the fuck did you crawl out of?"

"I was a passenger on the ship you just acquired. I take it you didn't read the captain's log. I was enjoying a lovely, restorative nap in one of their stasis capsules, not entirely by choice, when MJ woke me. He told me you were busy getting your rocks off with a human. I assumed he was delirious, but when repeated slaps to his head to jolt his synapses didn't change his story, I had to come see for myself."

Wearing a familiar scowl, Aramus growled. "Go away." It seemed sex hadn't cured his friend of his ornery nature. What a relief. One of Seth's enjoyments in life was antagonizing Aramus. The fights kept him fit.

As for leaving? No freaking way. "But you haven't even introduced us yet." Seth waggled his brows at the human, who bit her lip, probably so she wouldn't giggle. Mirth shone clearly in her eyes.

Aramus, however, seemed less than amused. "Who she is, is none of your business."

"Aw, come on, Aramus. Don't be like that. Aren't you just the teensiest, tiniest bit glad to see me?"

"Not really. It was a lot more quiet and peaceful with you gone."

Before Seth could reply, probably with something that would have really irritated Aramus, the dulcet tone of his wife interrupted. About time she'd caught him.

"Funny. I would have said the same thing myself." Anastasia crowded into Aramus' room, and while she flicked Seth a look, her gaze was snagged by the woman in the bed. Her voice couldn't hide its interest when she said, "If it isn't the forensic doctor. I've got questions for you."

"And I have a question too. Just who the fuck are you, lady, and what do you want?"

Ah, how sweet. His wife, who wanted to hate him and his best friend, who also pretended to hate him, were about to meet and probably hate each other. Seth beamed. Things were about to get truly interesting. "I think introductions are in order. Aramus, and hot-looking naked girl in his bed, I'd like you to meet Anastasia. My wife."

"Ex."

He couldn't let that pass unchallenged. "Now, darling, you know I don't believe in divorce."

"And I'm fine with becoming a widow." With those words, Anastasia, in a blur of movement, took Seth to the floor and held a gun to his head.

A wide grin stretched his lips wide. "Isn't she wonderful?" Now if only they were in a more private location and wearing fewer clothes.

"Would someone explain to me what the fuck is going on?" Aramus bellowed.

"It's a long story."

"Then download it to my BCI." The joys of cyborgs with wireless technology. To expedite matters, they let their chips do the talking. While Aramus processed the data, Anastasia released him with a whispered, "Point for me."

"Ha. I let you take me down. We both know who's the better fighter."

"You wish, golden boy."

"Is that a challenge?" Seth arched a brow, but before Anastasia could reply, Aramus, as usual, ruined the moment.

"Hey, annoying one, leave the nice lady alone."

"Nice? Wait until you get to know her. She's mean. Cut-throat. Always trying to one-up me and determined to make me look bad." How he loved her.

Aramus actually chuckled. Someone get a medic. There was something wrong with his friend! "Like I said, nice lady. But back to what you've just reported. It seems like you've been a busy boy. According to your memories, the scientist responsible for the drug that works on cyborgs was on board that ship we blew up."

"Unless he escaped."

"Nothing survived." Aramus said with unabashed glee.

"A shame," Anastasia replied. "I wouldn't have minded taking care of Jerry myself. The files on his and Stanley's computers too would have been useful."

"We downloaded what we could, but it's far from complete, and some of it is ciphered."

"I might be able to help with that. Here's to hoping you got the transmission logs. After our capture, I'd like to see who Jerry and Stanley contacted. Cyborgs of our caliber don't come along often, and I know the company would have special instructions for our capture."

"Think highly of yourself, do you?" Aramus couldn't help his sneer.

Seth let his wife handle it.

"Yes I do. Unlike you, I am much more than a simple soldier model."

Seth braced himself for fireworks. But, once again, the stranger in Aramus' body surprised him by laughing. "I'm happy being a grunt. It beats being an annoyingly human dickwad like Seth over there."

His wife shot him an amused glance. "You have a point. But back to my original theory. Someone would have been told about our capture, just like a report of the drug would have been sent for the company to use. It's protocol with every breakthrough. While Seth shook off its effect easily—"

"It's hard to bring down idiots with no brains."

"—I, on the other hand, apparently lacking some of his more recent upgrades, did succumb."

"Speaking of succumb, the soldiers I dealt with, while temporarily in their custody, had some of those new Taser weapons as well," Aramus informed them.

"Ah yes, the Tasers. Somewhat crude in nature, but again, with the simpler models, effective in forcing a reboot, which gives the military time to either restrain or dispose of cyborg units."

"Making them easier to experiment on," Aramus extrapolated.

"Indeed, as I'm sure your lady friend, Riley has told you."

"You know Aramus' girlfriend?" Seth interjected.

"I know of her. Those co-ordinates I told you to give Joe were for the planet Riley was imprisoned on. I assume you found the cyborgs there."

"We found some," Aramus replied. "Not many. Avion was there."

"He's alive!" Seth couldn't hide a note of surprise.

"Barely. They did quite the number on him."

"But he'll heal."

Aramus' face turned darker than usual, which didn't bode well.

Despite his certainty he wouldn't like the answer, Seth forced himself to ask, "What's wrong with Avion?"

"They turned off his nanos."

"They what?" Seth slapped the side of his head, then stuck a finger in his ear and waggled it.

"What are you doing?"

"I think my hearing malfunctioned. I thought you said his nanos weren't working."

"They aren't. MJ says he's healing at a slightly better rate than a human for the moment, but, without the nanos, it's only a matter of time before his parts start failing."

Something very much like fear gripped him. This was serious news. "We have to fix him."

"No shit. Problem is we don't know how. Reboots of his operating system have failed. As have blood transfusions."

"Of course it didn't work. Nanos are cyborg oriented," Seth mused aloud. "Else they would act like a virus taking over any live organism it came into contact with."

"Tell me something I don't know," Aramus snapped.

"I'll bet you didn't know that I have a heart-shaped mole on my left ass cheek."

Aramus shot him a glower. "We don't have time for me to kick your ass right now."

"While I would usually take you up on your challenge and enjoy the exercise, you are right. We have no time to waste. Avion must be fixed."

"No shit. Problem is we haven't the slightest idea how to begin."

"And the people who might have had a clue are all dead," Anastasia concluded. "Or, if they're not dead, then they're buried in some company facility."

Seth rubbed his chin. "So we need to find some scientists, or get him back to Einstein."

"I don't know if we have that kind of time. They fucked him up good."

"What about placing him in one of the cryo capsules," Anastasia suggested.

"We could try, but it's a temporary measure at best."

"But better than doing nothing. We need to find out where they were shipping us and get our hands on some scientists."

"I agree, but first we're going to need to tell Joe about everything that's happened. Given the fact your wife's cover was blown, our planet is most likely compromised."

"I did my best to keep it safe," Anastasia protested.

"But your best wasn't enough. Apparently you weren't as smart as you thought. How else do you explain your lover fucking you over?"

Seth didn't like Aramus' tone. "Watch it, dude. That's my wife you're talking to."

"I don't give a fuck. The fact remains that in fetching you for her revenge mission she put the whole planet at risk."

Anastasia hung her head. "Sorry."

"We can still fix this." Seth paced the room as he furiously tried to think of a way to salvage events.

"How? If you ask me, there's only one real solution if we ever want peace. Time to wipe out humanity, something I've been saying for years," Aramus snapped. Then, as if recalling whom he cuddled, amended, "I mean eradicate the military and company asshats."

"Hold onto your metal hate there, psycho bot. No need to get so radical." Anastasia waved a red flag at Aramus, but the little human kept him in check with a simple hand to his arm. "What we really need is to even the playing field."

Seth glanced at his wife, who bore a pensive expression. "Do you have an idea?" he asked.

"What if we could get our hands on the cloaking technology? Do you think this Einstein fellow you talked about could use it to hide the settlement?"

"Are you saying you know where to get it?" Aramus perked up, which meant, instead of a glower, he wore just a scowl.

"Yes. Kind of. It's how I bribed Seth to get him to help me."

"She lies. She promised me sex." Yeah, he totally deserved her jab to the stomach, but he wasn't about to admit he'd have helped her for free.

"The cloaking technology might possibly work. And, even if we can't use it to hide the colony, we could definitely equip our ships with it. Where is it?"

"Yeah, that's where we have a slight problem. I originally planned to have one of the equipped science vessels *disappear*." She made air quotes. "But someone blew them up."

Aramus drew his brows together and grumbled, "It wasn't my fault this time. The humans set off the bomb."

"Let's not play the blame game." Because Seth never fared well when it came down to facts. "Let's look for solutions. Obviously, those weren't the only vessels with the technology."

"No, but they were the ones I had access to. Give me a few hours and a steady network channel, and I can tell you which other ones have the new technology, and we can go get ourselves one."

"Forget getting our hands on a ship. Why aren't we going after the factory building them?" Seth asked. "I, for one, think we should even the odds by ridding them of the advantage they have."

Anastasia paused her pacing and planted her hands on her hips. That didn't bode well. "Great plan except for one thing."

"Which is?"

"From all indications, the factory to create the cloaking device is on earth."

Seth clapped his hands together and with a voice rife with glee said, "Whoo-eee! We're going to raid our home world. I call shotgun!"

Chapter Twenty-one

Having a naked man, with half his skull a gleaming dull metal, jump out of bed screaming, "You expect us to fucking invade the company on its home turf? Are you out of your nano-bleeping mind?" was slightly disturbing. Finding herself stepping between the ridiculously muscled, bare-assed male and her idiotic husband, who was laughing, with a sternly said, "Don't hurt my husband," was insane. Aramus would probably flatten her, given he probably outweighed her by a few hundred pounds—soldier models were built with more reinforced limbs and, thus, possessed greater weight.

However, the most astonishing part was the speed with which Seth, the ultimate jokester, took Aramus to the ground, immobilized him, and, in the deadliest tone she'd ever heard from him, said, "If you ever harm a single hair on her head, I will permanently kill you."

How totally unnecessary, given she was the one who intentionally stood in the bullish cyborg's way. How perversely romantic. What a waste of time. "Oh would you knock it off."

"For your information, I wasn't going to touch her," Aramus snapped. "I don't hurt women, even ones dumb enough to try and protect you. However, you, on the other hand, could use a few slaps to the head."

"What for?"

"For your bloody half-baked suggestion we raid an earth facility."

"What's wrong with my idea?"

"Because, even you have to admit, going to earth, even for the cloaking technology, is bloody nuts."

Seth grinned. "Probably. I'd even go so far as to call it suicidal. But, if that's where the factory is situated, then it makes the most sense. Unless there's another facility?" He glanced at Anastasia.

She shrugged. "Not that I know of."

"And is there any other way of getting the technology?" Seth asked.

"There was until tinman here blew it up."

"It self-destructed."

"Whatever. The fact remains we no longer have access to it unless we go to the source."

Aramus sighed. "I don't like it when you act rationally."

"Blame it on my wife. She brings out the best in me."

"If that's your best, then you have serious issues," she muttered.

He grinned. "You say the sweetest things."

Aramus gagged. "If you're done making me want to jam a screwdriver in my ear, can we get back to business? Do you have co-ordinates for this so-called cloak-making factory?"

"Not exactly. The secret is closely guarded. All I know is ships go into the dockyard for maintenance, disappear for a few months, and when they return, they have the new hardware installed."

"Back up a second, blondie. In other words, you don't know where it is. So why say earth?"

"Because it makes the most sense. The ships disappear while docked planet-side and reappear there. I've also been tracking military and company space routes for the past year now. Those ships don't appear to be leaving earth to get the modifications."

"Or they're hiding it well."

"Possibly." She shrugged.

"Do you think this mysterious facility might also be hiding the cyborg origin?" Seth asked.

"Again a possibility. Given the secrecy behind it all, I'd say there's even a possibility we could find the head of the company." A viperous head that needed chopping.

"Your target." Seth stated the obvious.

"Yes."

Seth played devil's advocate. "But how will you know him? Whoever runs the company never shows his face. We could talk to him face to face and never know it's him."

"I'll know." Where the certainty came from she couldn't have said, but deep in her gut, what human instinct remained to her, she knew she'd recognize the source behind the ultimate evil.

"I am less concerned about her vendetta than I am about finding this fucking joint," Aramus snapped. "Any ideas on how we will find this place. We don't even have a name for the company. Hell, even its employees don't know it."

"Some do." Up until now, Riley had remained silent, but when she did finally speak, all eyes veered her way. The human, nervous at all the attention, blushed and ducked her head under their sudden perusal.

"You know the name?" Forget hiding the surprise in her query. Anastasia had long wondered why the company, who had so many fingers dipped in so many places, never seemed to have an actual identity.

"Maybe. Like you said, everyone calls it the company, but once, when I was in my cell after one of my, um, beatings," Aramus growled at Riley's admission, "I thought I heard Dennison call it by a name. He talked about a corporation titled Advenus."

Seth frowned. "That doesn't sound familiar."

Perhaps not to him, but Anastasia certainly recalled hearing it once or twice before. Of more interest, the memory of it was hazy, which meant she wasn't supposed to know. "I think the doctor here might be on to something. I know I've heard that term before."

"In that case, we'll have to get Einstein to start digging. If there is anything public under that name, or even not so public, he'll find it. So who's game to go on a mission?"

Aramus didn't immediately volunteer. He looked to the human.

Apparently that bothered Seth because he said, "Since when don't you jump on the chance to wreak mayhem? Have I entered an alternate realm?"

"Perhaps I finally learned that there's more to life than vengeance."

Seth clasped his hands to his heart. "I think I'm dying. My best friend, the most murderous cyborg alive, doesn't want to kill humans. Is it me, or does nothing make sense anymore?"

"Stop it," Anastasia hissed.

Her rebuke didn't stop Seth from harassing Aramus, who ignored him to have a discussion with his girlfriend.

"It would be dangerous," Aramus said to Riley.

"Yes, but the company has to be stopped. We can't keep letting them do this, Aramus." The fragile human put her hand on his arm, and Anastasia could see the shock on Seth's face when the big brute's expression softened.

"I don't suppose you'd let me put you somewhere safe."

"I belong by your side," Riley bravely replied.

"Then, I'll do my best to protect you," the big guy replied.

"Hot damn, Aramus is in love. I call being best man!" Seth slung an arm around Aramus and beamed.

"You'll be called dead man if you don't get your arm off me," Aramus snapped.

"Can you kill him after the mission?" Anastasia asked. "He might be useful, given we'll need to sneak in, and of all the cyborgs I've known, he's one of the few who could pull it off."

A glower creased Aramus' face. "Sneak? I hate sneaking. Sneaking leads to ambushes, which leads to shooting, which leads to mayhem. On second thought, I like sneaking. Sneak away. Or we could just try the direct approach. They might not expect that."

"Remind me to leave bucket head behind when we go topside," Anastasia said.

"Who you calling a bucket you bleached blonde hussy?" Aramus growled.

"Let's ditch the name calling and see whose training is better." She goaded him with beckoning fingers.

Before they could tango, Seth wrapped a steel band around both of them and beamed. "How sweet. My wife and BF are having their first fight. This day just keeps getting better and better."

"Your friend is an idiot. We can't just go barging in and expect to make it back out alive," Anastasia said, trying to be the voice of reason.

"Why ever not? I'm still here, aren't I?" Aramus boasted.

"Says the guy with the metal head."

"That wasn't from a mission."

"Yeah, a girl did that to him," Seth piped in.

"I don't really care. Although, if the lady in question would like lessons on shooting to kill, send her my way. I'd be more than happy to help her amend her shot."

"Hey, that's not nice," Riley exclaimed.

"Neither is he. But, come on, you're talking about a highly guarded company facility where they're developing alien technology and who knows what else," she exclaimed.

"Alien? There's that word again. Do you know something I don't, wifey poo?" Seth crossed his arms and arched a brow at her.

For a highly evolved male, he could be awfully dense. "I do. You just seem to have a hard time grasping the hints. As I've already told you, aliens are real."

"Bullshit! I thought you were yanking my metal chain."

"Not bull, but alien shit. And alien artifacts. I'm not one hundred percent sure, but I'd wager heavily that the cloaking technology and some of the stuff the company is working on isn't of their own making. Or did you really think they came up with the nanotechnology themselves?"

The shocked expression on the male cyborg faces said it all. The human however? She didn't seem surprised. "You knew that already?" Anastasia accused.

Riley shrugged. "I've suspected it since I got to know Aramus and the others. It makes the most sense. Given the way the company is researching and experimenting, it makes me think they found something and used it without fully understanding it."

"Area 51 conspiracies are alive and well," Seth announced.

"Area 51 happened. Problem was their lack of knowledge and equipment at the time led to them destroying all the viable samples and technology that crash landed. They weren't so foolish the second time," Anastasia told them. "From conversations I've overhead, and pieced together, I believe they managed to preserve some of the DNA and recover an alien craft. It's the most logical conclusion as to where the cloaking technology and new metal we're seeing crop up is coming from."

"Descended from aliens. Now that is freaking cool!" Only Seth would think of it that way.

"You've seen these aliens?" Aramus asked her.

Anastasia shook her head. "No. No one has. What about your doctor friend?"

"I've just seen some of the results on my autopsy table of what seems to be attempts to splice humans with alien DNA."

"Splices which wouldn't work. I seem to recall hearing something about the ET's being water based."

"Are you sure about that? I mean them being water based?" Riley asked.

"No. It's just conjecture. Why do you ask?"

"Because the stuff I saw in the lab, the alien stuff, it definitely wasn't from some water-based ET. Do you think it's possible the company has found a second set of life?"

"Two aliens?" Even Seth sounded scoffing.

Riley bit her lip and dropped her head, but Anastasia wanted to hear more. "Why do you think that? And I, unlike my idiot husband, am asking quite seriously. Like I said, I only heard rumors of a water based alien, and through the same gossip mill about gray aliens with spiny backs. I just assumed they were one and the same."

"I guess they could be."

"But you don't seem to think so?" Anastasia prodded.

Riley bit her lip before shaking her head. "The kind of genetic modifications I saw weren't from something that spent extended periods of time in the water. If I had to guess, I would have said the aliens were from an arid planet. Not only that but they share a DNA close enough to ours to splice."

"We need to find out more," announced Aramus, who'd dressed while they conversed, Seth providing cover with his body, acting the part of jealous husband.

"Hey, do you think having alien nanos would explain my love of probing things?" Seth leered at her.

Anastasia restrained a sigh. Nope. Seth hadn't changed. Still a jokester, but a loveable one who was going to get his ass handed to him if he didn't start taking things seriously. Time to change the course of this conversation. "If we're going to infiltrate the company on earth, we're going to need help from the surface."

"And just who would be crazy enough to do that?" Aramus asked with a snort.

"Why, the movement for the ethical treatment of cybernetic organisms of course," Anastasia announced. "Lucky for us, I happen to know their leader, Adam."

"Know him how?" Seth asked. "And how do you know we can trust him?"

Nothing like a little excitement to spark a lively conversation. Anastasia lit the fuse. "Adam is a cyborg, and my ex-boyfriend."

Kaboom!

Chapter Twenty-two

Manhandling his wife perhaps wasn't the most mature of responses, but when he heard the word ex-boyfriend and found out he was a cyborg? Irrational or not, Seth kind of lost it.

He bellowed, "I'm going to kill the bastard," to which she replied, "Good luck, he's also a spy model, and bigger than you." To add insult to injury, Aramus laughed and said, "Suckah!", which was so totally unexpected that Seth just about had a meltdown.

And then Anastasia's words really penetrated. "Bigger than me? As in size or *size?*" he demanded, his brows drawing together in a frown.

"Does size really matter? I did end up dumping him if it's any consolation."

Not really. So over his shoulder she went, protesting all the way. She obviously didn't mind too much, else she could have gotten out of his fireman hold. Any half-trained idiot could, but she let him carry her while trying to placate him. "Now, Seth, husband, there's no need to be so irrational. Yes, Adam and I dated after our breakup during the revolution, but ultimately we parted ways."

"Because you hated each other?"

"No, more because I needed to go off-planet to follow some leads. We left on good terms."

"And this is supposed to make me feel better how?" he snarled, stomping to his old quarters on board.

"Because if I ask him to help us, he probably will."

"But I don't want his help." Petulant? Yes. He wouldn't deny it. He didn't care if this other cyborg shared some of the same nanos and experience. He didn't give a flying fuck if he could help them. Seth didn't want this guy, this bigger guy, anywhere near *his* wife.

"Oh stop being such a baby about this. We need his aid. Why are you so opposed to it?"

"Isn't it obvious? He's seen you naked."

"So? Other women saw you naked too," she reminded. "You don't see me going all batshit crazy."

"What if I told you one of them was on board right now, what would you say?"

Yup. Like he'd thought, she let him manhandle her because he'd no sooner taunted her than he found himself on his back with a gun pointed at his head.

"Where is the slut?" she snarled.

"Jealous much?" he asked.

"Just point me in her direction. I have a cure."

With her snapping eyes, curled lip, and intense expression promising deadly retribution, she looked beyond gorgeous. How he loved her, even if she had jealousy issues. "I lied. My encounters were of the paid-for variety." Mostly. But none of them meant anything and, now that Anastasia was back in his life, would never happen again.

She tucked her gun away and rose to her feet. "I hate you."

"But not as much as you love me," he said with a grin.

"Do not."

"Sure you do." He winked, knowing it would aggravate her. It did. So cute. "By the way, I meant to ask, how the hell did you get your hands on a gun? Don't tell me MJ armed you?"

"Not exactly. You know how I hate to be unarmed." She shrugged. "I kind of took it from another one of your shipmates when I went chasing after you."

"You didn't kill him, did you?" Wife or not, if she murdered another cyborg, it probably wouldn't go over well.

"No, I didn't kill him. I actually didn't have to use any violence at all." How disgruntled she seemed. "When I explained I needed his weapon to murder you, he handed it over. Said to tell you Aphelion says hi."

A snort of laughter escaped him. "That sly little fucker. I knew he had a sense of humor buried in that serious body of his somewhere. But we've digressed from our original problem. You slept with this Adam dude."

"And?"

"I don't like it." He admitted it. Given the lies that had come between them before, he saw no reason to hold back the truth. Perhaps had they both been more open in the past, they would have never gotten to the point they had in the first place.

"That makes no sense. Adam and I broke up a while ago, so I don't get why you would have a problem with it, especially since while I was dating Jerry you didn't seem to give two hoots."

He couldn't help but make a disparaging noise. "Ha. Jerry was a human. I knew he couldn't compare to my awesomeness."

"Says you."

"Knows me."

"I dare you to prove it." She planted her hands on her hips and her lips curled into a smirk of challenge.

"Excuse me, but are you daring me to show you, in person, just how awesome I am?"

"I'm sorry. Did your higher brain functions get damaged from too many slaps to the head? That's exactly what I'm saying. And, since you're having problems with your comprehension skills, let me explain it in simple terms. I would like you to prove it to me while naked. I also want you to make it exciting, and I do expect a screaming orgasm for the finale."

A mortal man would have fallen to his knees in worship before such a demand. As it was, Seth's BCI practically melted from the overload of his circuits as he swept her into his arms and ran the rest of the way to his quarters.

He couldn't have said how their clothes ended up on the floor, although picking up the shreds later, he could vaguely recall some ripping of fabric amidst panting kisses.

Forget thinking logically. Forget taking his time and savoring the moment. Passion consumed him. And hunger. A hunger for her flesh.

Having placed her upon his bed, her body naked and splayed for his visual feasting, he admired her, memorized every inch, replacing his old memories of her with the new. She'd changed little on the outside, and yet, with them starting afresh, he felt a need to re-catalogue everything he knew about her, starting with her beautiful face. With her eyes half open, the lids heavy with desire, her cheeks a slight pink, meaning she'd let her body controls loose, and her lips swollen and juicy, she took his higher thinking process away. No other woman could ever compare, not for him.

He let his gaze wander, dipping down to her breasts, perfect, round globes with sweet puckered nipples. His already hard cock pulsed at the sight, but it pearled at the glimpse of the moist haven between her thighs.

"I can't believe you dyed it blonde," he murmured.

"All part of my cover. It's also easier than keeping it shaved," she replied with a naughty smile.

"I like the new hairdo, but I'll admit, I preferred the original."

"Then perhaps it's time I went back to being a brunette. With my cover blown, there's no reason why I can't."

There she was again, implying that his wishes mattered. Could it be she was changing her mind about the two of them staying together? Did he dare hope?

He'd worry about it later. With the sensual feast spread before him, he had more important things to attend to, such as bringing her so much pleasure she'd never even want to look at another male again.

Suddenly impatient, he covered her body with his, her softer, toned frame the perfect complement to his sleek lines. He shuddered at the skin-to-skin contact, savoring it. Never mind he'd touched and explored her during their trip out to the military ship. Now, things were different. Now, he could see the possibility of a future. Something in her had changed. *I do believe she's ready to stop fighting and to try again.* Which meant she sought to control. Theirs ever had been a war of who would prevail. Her arms twined around his neck, her fingers laced through his hair, and she drew his mouth to hers, engaging him in a passion-filled kiss.

Let her think she called the shots. He'd still make her scream first. Maybe twice.

Catching her bottom lip between his teeth, he tugged before sucking it. She squirmed under him, hips grinding and pressing her moist sex against his cock, which was trapped between their bodies.

"So impatient," he murmured against her mouth as he untangled her arms from around his neck and pushed them over her head. Wanting to dominate the situation or not, she moaned at his manhandling. In public, she might act tough and bitchy, but when naked in his arms, she liked it when he used his superior strength against her.

Anchoring her hands with one of his, which she could have broken free of but didn't, he went exploring. His lips traveled the sensitive skin of her neck down to the valley between her breasts. He buried his face, inhaling the unique scent that was hers alone. With his one free hand, he cupped a firm globe, squeezing it until she moaned. Leaving the heavenly valley, he shifted his head to latch on to her protruding nipple. With the hard nub caught between his lips, he sucked and swirled his tongue around the engorged tip, delighting in the way she writhed and mewled.

And people thought cyborgs didn't feel. He begged to differ. Cyborgs felt all too much, when they chose.

Even the simplest of acts, like him blowing on the wet nub, had her gasping and arching her upper body. So fucking beautiful.

But it seemed wrong to lavish all of his attention on just the one berry. He switched over to the other nipple, giving it the same passionate attention. Back and forth he played, an enjoyable game of drive his wife nuts, a game he could have easily conducted for hours, but another pleasure zone awaited him. And, by the way her hips thrust and the way she panted, she was more than ready for him to switch his focus.

Down her body he slid, his hand still gripping hers, holding her a willing prisoner. He pulled them from over her head to rest on her stomach to make it easier for him to indulge in his new objective.

Her legs parted, giving him plenty of space to nestle himself and give his lips access to the most sensitive part of her. Her entire body shuddered as he blew on her sex. How the scent of her arousal titillated. He wanted to bury his face against her pubes and just breathe her in, savor the richness of her desire. Instead, he gave her one long lick, letting the taste of her sit on his tongue, an explosion of flavor that he filed under the term ambrosia.

"Seth." She moaned his name, and a shiver went through him. Experience wasn't something he lacked, not when it came to women, and yet, no one ever made him feel like Anastasia did. No one could make him lose control. Make him forget who and what he was. Make him feel *alive*.

Forget teasing her. It was more like torture, for them both. He let his hunger take over and feasted on her sweetness. Tasted her sweet pussy. Spread her velvety pink lips and let his tongue rediscover the wonders of her flesh.

She went wild. His beautiful controlled wife bucked and writhed under his oral assault. She cried out his name. She heaved, she thrust, she begged. With her enhanced strength, he had no choice but to release her hands but only so he could anchor her hips, pinning her for the tongue-lashing he was determined to give. Forcing her to feel his tongue as it plunged into her sex. Feel as he flicked it across her clit. Scream as he bit down on her most sensitive spot.

As he sucked and nibbled at her clit, Anastasia came, tremors of bliss rocking her sex, tremors he felt on his tongue when he plunged it between her damp folds.

But even when the shakes and shudders of her body slackened, he didn't relent. They weren't done. Far from it. He went back to his pleasurable task of teasing her. Tasting her. Bringing her back to the blissful edge. When she panted his name, over and over, "Seth, please. Seth, now. Se-e-eth," he finally stopped his oral play and allowed himself to slide up her body until they were face to face again.

"Look at me," he demanded.

He didn't have to ask twice. Even with her lids passion swollen, she gazed at him. In that moment, she couldn't hide what she felt. Couldn't hide her need for him. Couldn't hide her love. Couldn't hide her vulnerability.

All things he recognized because he felt them too. "I love you, Anastasia. I always have. I always will. You are the only one for me."

Her hands cupped his cheeks. "And I love you. Forever and always."

Which for cyborgs could mean a very long time. Was it wrong to want to fist pump at a time like this?

Probably, especially since he was braced on his forearms, the tip of his cock nudging her moist sex. Forget easing his way in to that snug channel. She locked legs of steel around his shanks and drove him in.

"Fucking yeah!" Perhaps not the most romantic thing he could have said, but then again, could anything really describe the intensely pleasurable sensation of being buried so deep within the woman he loved? Hell, he was so overcome by the bombarding sensations, both physical and emotional, that he couldn't help but close his eyes to truly savor it. *She loves me. She wants me.* She was also wet, tight, and still slightly quivering from her first orgasm. Control? What was control? Where his wife was concerned, he didn't have any. Instead, he felt as though he was in a race, a race where neither wanted to finish first. A race where a tie was the best win of all.

Teeth gritted, he battled the waves of pleasure threatening to overcome him, determined to bring her along with him when he went over the cliff. Sink, pull back, thrust, retreat. Each motion was a delight and a step closer to bliss. The head of his penis butted against her G-spot, and each time he struck, she clamped down tighter, and tighter. Exquisite didn't come close to describing it.

"Faster," she urged. "Harder."

Had he mentioned how perfect she was? Their bodies moved in sync, her legs, still locked around his shanks, giving him no choice. As if he'd move away now!

Her panting cries grew more frantic, his breathing ragged. A flush enveloped them both, and when her climax hit, so did euphoria. As she let out a keening scream and clenched her channel around his cock, he shuddered himself, unable to hold back. He gave a final thrust, sinking balls deep before spurting wetly inside her.

He said the words that sang in his heart. "I love you," and she replied with a sensual, "Ditto."

Chapter Twenty-three

Anastasia would admit she hadn't replied in the most romantic fashion after his second declaration. She couldn't, even if she felt it. Never mind she'd told him during the throes of sex, during the cool down, reality reasserted itself. While she'd gotten over the misunderstandings of the past and come to the realization she still loved Seth, and would lay down her life for his, she still couldn't let go of her primary mission, her one goal in life.

To see the man responsible for her cybernetic state pay for his crimes—in other words, die, while screaming, preferably with lots of bloodshed. What she didn't expect was for Seth to agree to help her, after his mini meltdown.

"Ditto? Ditto!" Seth dumped her on the bed so he could jump to his feet, six feet plus of naked splendor pacing in a confined space. It was visually entertaining. "Is that all you have to say?"

"Fine. I care for you."

"Says the girl who said she loved me not even five minutes ago during sex."

He would bring that up. She sprang from the bed feeling at a disadvantage and scrounged through his meager closet for something to wear. "I never meant to imply I didn't, but I can't abandon everything I've worked toward these last few years just to be with you."

"Who is asking you to?" He paused in his pacing to direct his laser-blue gaze on her.

"I'm sorry. I'm confused. Don't you want to be with me again?"

"Yes."

"But being with me means ditching Joe and the others, especially if they don't agree with our plan to meet up with the rebel cyborg alliance on earth."

"If they don't like it, then they can make plans without me."

"What do you mean Joe and the others can make plans without you?" She paused in her dressing, the borrowed garments not exactly the most seductive of items given the T-shirt was a few sizes too large and the pants baggy in the ass and requiring a roll of the cuffs so they wouldn't drag on the floor.

"Is your cognizant chip malfunctioning?" he replied with a quirk of a brow. "It means, even if Joe doesn't agree, I am still going on this mission. We'll meet up with this jerk you used to date, use him to get us into this factory or research lab or wherever it is they make these ships, and take what we need."

"And after?"

"What do you mean after?"

"My primary goal still remains finding the head of the company. What if we don't find him there?"

Seth reached out and grabbed her hands, enveloping them in his and forcing her to face him, his expression serious. "If we don't find him, then we keep looking. However long it takes. Which means, even once we get the cloaking technology into the hands of my brothers and friends, where you go, I go."

"But I thought—"

"Thought what? That after finding you again I'd ever want you to leave my sight? Not happening, gorgeous. Meeting our creator obviously means a lot to you. And, oddly enough, I find myself curious too. Curious and not averse to the idea of meting out some punishment. While I don't entirely hate my state of being, I mean being a cyborg after all does have its perks, I don't like the way they went about it, or the methods they used. I think they could have achieved many of the same results if they'd only asked. Plenty of humans would have volunteered to become super men and women. So, yes, I do want to look the a-hole in the eye and ask him why."

"But what about Joe and the others? I thought they needed you."

"They do, but I'm not so vain as to realize that others can step into my shoes. They probably won't wear them as well, or appear as dashing, but that's the problem with trying to replace perfection."

"Perfection?"

His eyes twinkled with mischief. "You disagree? Because I thought I recalled someone mumbling something along the lines of 'oh my god.' That, to me, implies greatness."

"Or a problem with my programming. It's been a while since my last maintenance check."

"You are not defective, gorgeous. Just in love."

She made a moue. "I guess." The expression on his face made her laugh. "Okay fine. I'll admit it.

I love you, even if you are a goof. So are we really going to track down the son of a bitch behind the origin of the cyborgs?"

"Track him down. Make him pay. And, if we're lucky, show the world that we're not the monsters they've made us out to be."

"Maybe we'll even find this mysterious source of all cyborgs like you've hinted at."

"The source? What source?" His brows drew together in a puzzled frown.

She pursed her lips. How could he have forgotten? He was the one who'd told her about the source, something she could still only vaguely recollect. Cyber units never forgot anything—unless something in their programming made them. What was it about this source that— She blinked and opened her mouth, only to shut it. *What was I about to say?*

"Cat got your tongue?" he teased.

"I'd prefer if a certain spy I knew took it."

And there went her second set of borrowed garments, from covering her one moment to tattered rags the next. Ah well. She could cobble another ensemble together later. Right now, she had more important things to do, such as making up for lost time with her husband.

Her initial mission might not have gone the way she planned, and the future remained uncertain, but, as Seth said, later while she lay cocooned in his arms, "From here on out, we will face whatever the universe throws at us, together." Words she clutched with all her mechanical heart.

Of course, being Seth, he had to ruin the moment. "Well together except for when we meet this guy Adam. Him, I want to spend some time alone with so we can *discuss* his association with my wife."

Lucky her, life would never be boring again. Or lonely. *I've got a second chance at happiness, and this time, I'm not letting anyone fuck it up.*

Epilogue

To Seth's relief, he didn't have to make an actual choice between his wife and his friends. Once apprised of the situation and the newest events, Joe approved of their plan to invade the earth facility creating the cloaking devices, because as their leader so eloquently put it, "We need to fuck over the bastards and even the odds."

However, a trip to earth, while exciting, required careful planning. They couldn't just fly into restricted air space and expect to land without anyone taking notice. What they could expect according to the hypothetical models they ran was to get their asses shot down. However, where there was a cyborg will, there was a way. Somehow they'd find a way to make it to the surface and find this group for the ethical treatment of cyborgs. And find Adam.

However, that aspect of their mission was only part of the virtual meeting they held in the control center of the *SSBiteMe*. Much had happened since Seth had left his cyborg home world. Aramus' mission had recovered some cyborgs. Anastasia had also increased their population by one, and the intel they both brought to the holographic table blew more than a few circuit boards, at least in those present for the meeting.

The announcement of alien life being responsible for the new technology and possibly their origin caused a stunned silence.

Of about two seconds.

"I knew it! I fucking knew it!" Kyle crowed. "I am like superman, only without the tights, and forget kryptonite. Metal makes me stronger!"

No one begrudged Aramus the slap he gave Kyle across the back of the head.

It took a few moments for Joe to regain control. "All of this is very interesting and gives us a new direction in which to look. Despite the possibility of our location being compromised, I don't think we should move quite yet. Einstein's been working on the cloaking issue baffling our sensors and has come up with some innovative ways of combatting it. We've also begun dispersing the population and dismantling some of our key installations. I've got the cyborgs spreading out over the continent and onto some of the nearby planets to ensure we're not sitting ducks waiting to get picked off."

"Great counter measures, especially once you add in Einstein's plan to seed trip alarms in the air space leading to the planet, but we still need the cloaking tech if we want to move from a defensive position to an offensive one," Seth pointed out.

His image wavering as the signal fluttered, Joe nodded. "I agree. We need to see what we can do about not only getting our hands on it but also destroying the installation where it's made so the military and the company can't use it."

A certain brash cyborg showed an interest at this point, now that the talk had gone from blah blah recap to actual action. "Did someone say we needed to blow some shit up? I'm in," Aramus volunteered.

"I kind of figured you would be. However, this operation requires stealth and finesse. Seth and Anastasia, I want you to be in charge of that part of the mission. In other words, you sneak in, get the intel we need and then get out before Aramus turns the factory into a crater."

"Fucking A!" Aramus actually did a fist pump, which left more than one mouth hanging open.

But dead silence prevailed when Joe added, "I'd also like you to bring along Avion."

"Me?"

"Him?"

The surprise in the room could almost be felt. "Yes, I want you to bring Avion. Avion, you know firsthand what the company was up to. Your knowledge might be invaluable."

"No offense," Anastasia interrupted. "But you're talking about bringing a blind cyborg on a mission of stealth."

"I know. Not exactly ideal, but I've talked it over with Einstein. He doesn't know if he can help Avion. However, there is a chance this installation might have a cure. They figured out how to turn the nanos off, so maybe they know how to turn them back on. And as we all know, Avion needs to turn on his nanos if he wants to survive."

The sobering reminder that their cyborg friend was currently in a race against death sobered them all. Cyborg technology wasn't worth shit without the nanos to back it up. Bit by bit, Avion's body would shut down. They had time, but not much, to save his life.

"Talk about bringing the party down. I can tell even without eyes that you're all feeling sorry for me. Don't. I'm tough. It will take more than a few unresponsive bots in my bloodstream to bring me down. Let's worry more about getting our hands on the cloaking device." Brave words. Avion's smile and attempt to lighten the mood only served to highlight his frail health.

"Oh shut the fuck up you altruistic bastard. We're going to save your ass just so I can kick it," Aramus rumbled.

"I've already set a course for earth," Aphelion announced.

"Excellent, however, you'll only be doing a drop-off of Seth, Anastasia and Avion." Joe held up his hand before Aramus could protest. "Before you blow a gasket, rest assured that you will probably be needed to blow the place up, but while we give our landing team a chance to do their job, I've got a different mission in mind for you. Judging by the reports you gave me and some information I got elsewhere, I might have found the location for at least one of the aliens we suspect the company has gotten their hands on. I need you to find them."

"And do what? Ask them to hand over their technology or I'll blow them up?" Aramus asked hopefully.

"I'd prefer you try and form a treaty instead of engaging us in another war on a different front if you don't mind, which is why Aphelion is going as your second and Kyle as our interspecies relations officer."

"Woo hoo! A promotion." The second smack to Kyle's skull went unchallenged as well.

"Anybody got anything else they want to say?" Joe looked at everyone around the virtual table.

If he expected dissension, he wouldn't find it. There wasn't a cyborg in that control center or back home who wouldn't lay down his life for the good of the colony and all cyber units universe wide. And it went without saying that they all had a burning desire to find out more about their origin. Born of a human mother and father, reborn of what?

That remained to be seen. With Anastasia by his side, Seth couldn't wait to find out. And plant his fist in this Adam's face.

Love might conquer all for humans, but he was cyborg, and no amount of programming could cure him of his impulse control, or jealousy.

Bring on the adventure and danger. Booyah!

*

Elsewhere...

The walls of her prison never changed. Dull metal all around, a lead compound with no conducting abilities, smooth as glass, impermeable to all attempts to gouge or scratch. It also blocked all attempts to call for help. It was the perfect prison. A cell no one could escape from, not even a cyborg.

Light did not exist in this space. The only sounds were those of her own making. She had spent an eternity alone. Or so it seemed. Her internal clock said it had been nine months, seven days, six hours, and five seconds since the last time they'd checked on her. But did time matter when everything else seemed to stand still?

Am I mad yet? She should be.

Am I dead? Perhaps the silence and darkness meant she'd finally passed on.

Doubtful. Those who'd recreated her had built her too well. They'd defended her against all sorts of harm. Made her impregnable. Daddy's little girl, perfect in every way, except for one thing. In her father's quest to save her, he'd taken her humanity and freedom.

What was the use of being perfect if she couldn't be free?

But even if she were, what would she do? Where would she go? She was alone. Even Daddy had abandoned her in the end.

"You are no longer my daughter." And whose fault was that?

Once upon a time, that memory had the ability to hurt. That time had long passed. She no longer felt anything, just fatigue, not a bodily one, but one of the mind, not the spirit. Of that the scientists seemed certain. The term godless and without a soul had been applied. It seemed that being a cyborg, no matter her human origin, took away her soul.

No morals? No conscience? No soul? In that case then that meant no going to hell. She was free from the sins of humans. In reply to the scientists belief, she tore off their faces and limbs. Essentially anything that came within reach. It was messy. But fun.

Her rebellion had been sadly short-lived but even now, proved pleasant to reminisce upon.

The grating sound from above her saw her craning to peer upward. Had they finally solved the riddle of her existence? Did they finally have a solution to their problem of how to kill? They kept trying, but in the end, nothing worked. It was why Daddy had stuck her in the hole. *It's for your own good, sweetie.* She could see the lie, but she'd gone anyway. Why not? She had nothing better to do.

A bright light angled down, the proverbial white tunnel, or something else? Aliens coming to take me away?

She almost giggled.

I am mad. Mad as the hatter. Mad as the AI from that space movie. Crazy, crazy, nuts.

And alone. All alone.

Or was she? In the brief shining moment when someone called down and asked if she was still there—like duh, where else would she go?—a mind touched hers. A single mind out of hundreds. A single personality that actually *saw* her.

Who are you? he asked.

Good question. She no longer even remembered. All she had was the identity they'd given her. *I am known as One.* She didn't need to see him to perceive his puzzlement.

Where are you?
Hidden. A prisoner. One without hope.
There's always hope.

Not for me. How sad to admit to another, the first true contact she'd had in who knew how long.

Don't give up. I'll —

The contact was abruptly shattered as they slid the grate back over her prison.

And somewhere deep in space, a cyborg who tried to hold onto hope, even if all seemed lost, sat bolt upright in his bed. Heart pounding. Pulse racing. The end of his promise spoken aloud, "— find you."

The End until you dive back in to the cyborg world with Adam.

Made in the USA
Columbia, SC
17 June 2017